THE HIDDEN DRAGON

THE HIDDEN DRAGON

MELISSA MARR

NANCY PAULSEN BOOKS

NANCY PAULSEN BOOKS

An imprint of Penguin Random House LLC, New York

First published in the United States of America by Nancy Paulsen Books,
an imprint of Penguin Random House LLC, 2023

Visit us online at penguinrandomhouse.com.

Library of Congress Cataloging-in-Publication Data
Names: Marr, Melissa, author. | Title: The hidden dragon / Melissa Marr.
Description: New York: Nancy Paulsen Books, 2023. | Summary: "A sea-faring girl and her
friends take on pirates and grown-ups and bond with dragons as they work to make the
world a better place"—Provided by publisher.
Identifiers: LCCN 2022036104 | ISBN 9780525518556 (hardcover) | ISBN 9780525518563 (ebook)
Subjects: CYAC: Magic—Fiction. | Dragons—Fiction. | Gargoyles—Fiction. | Pirates—Fiction. |
Friendship—Fiction. | Sea stories. | Fantasy. | LCGFT: Fantasy fiction. | Novels.
Classification: LCC PZ7.M34788 Hi 2023 | DDC [Fic]—dc23
LC record available at https://lccn.loc.gov/2022036104

Printed in the United States of America

ISBN 9780525518556

1 3 5 7 9 10 8 6 4 2

BVG

Edited by Nancy Paulsen
Design by Eileen Savage | Text set in Skolar Latin

To all the kids (young and old) who dream of
exploring the sea, of meeting dragons,
or of changing the world.

THE HIDDEN DRAGON

PROLOGUE

◆——◆——◆

At first when the door between worlds opened, it was mostly the creatures that flew who went. Gargoyles crossed. Faeries crossed. Even a few dragonets crossed. The water things couldn't pass as easily—except for the kelpies. They needed only a teaspoon of water at a time to slip from world to world.

No logic to kelpies, shrinking themselves into a million droplets all hither and dither.

Marian did not shrink. She was what she was—no larger, no smaller. And she wasn't willing to scrape a single shimmering dragon scale against the doorway. It was simply not suitable for anyone with dignity to behave as the kelpies did, or for that matter, as dragonets did. They were both embarrassments in their way.

But then a few of the smaller ones went through the opening. And when Marian watched the flicker and flash of a hatchling darting through the door, she *had* to follow! None of her kind's hatchlings would be left alone in that new world. Marian would make sure of it.

The children were everything, and if they were not taken care of and adored, what was the point of *anything* else? Some types of creatures had nests they didn't tend. Other kinds of beings hovered over their own young but were hostile to young that weren't *theirs*. Marian, however, was certain that *all* young were precious—not *only* dragons. She took it upon herself to collect any hatchlings without parents. Her wings were large enough to shelter more than herself.

So Marian jabbed her claws into the door, and she tugged. A screech rippled through the sea. It was loud enough to embarrass Marian, but she kept moving.

Opening the door so very wide meant that many more sea creatures would pass through to the other side.

Dragon hatchlings tumbled through the gate in a great *whoosh*. Marian watched them stretch and grow in their new home, but she reminded herself that there were fish aplenty. There was also sea grass that grew in underwater forests. Plants reached as tall as the land dwellers' trees—and then grew higher still. Her kind would not want for food or space, despite the size they reached in this new water.

The only rule she set was that they must all be careful of the creatures of the land. One never knew what *they* were like. Dangerous things lived on land.

Soon many sea creatures frolicked and thrived in the deep, where they had food and safety. And in the very bottom of that deep dark water were sparkling, glimmering things that Marian began to gather. Sometimes they had to topple a ship to get the golden sparklies or the stone sparklies. That was easy enough. She was, after all, a dragon.

The only problem left for Marian was the Otter.

The sea dragons all heard the Otter's voice, and sometimes they couldn't resist going splashing to the surface to seek her out. It was dangerous, but Marian understood the impulse. She desperately wanted to be near the Otter again, too.

TWELVE YEARS LATER

CHAPTER 1

◆——◆——◆

London

London had every intention of buying passage out of Glass City. He carried his savings—gold coins and silver ones, a few bits of copper, and assorted gems—as well as a small bundle of clothes, as he set off toward the docks. London had been there often enough that his feet could find it even if his eyes were closed. Ships meant freedom, a new start, adventure. Who *wouldn't* dream of setting sail?

"This is the day!" London stepped to the edge of the dock, scanning quickly for kelpies. Getting eaten because he was careless would be a terrible start—and end—to his future.

Seeing no water horses rising to nibble passersby, London relaxed.

Birds' cries and people's voices mixed with the sounds of water lapping against hulls. Ships of all kinds cluttered the harbor. Personal boats and tall ships mixed with barges and tugs.

But when London spotted a relocation ship on the far end of

the dock—*not* the kind of ship he was hoping to board—he shivered. People who were a "burden on the empire" got shipped away, packed like fish in a barrel, to work in one of the wild lands the empire now owned. London remembered watching his mum being taken away on one of those. He liked to imagine her in a better place, teaching other kids in some foreign land, but he wasn't even sure if she'd survived the journey.

He'd stayed here at the docks that long-ago day, alone and hungry, until some kids found him. They took him with them, and that's how he ended up living underground.

Now a man's voice rang out: "You there, lad!"

It was one of the kingdom's patrol officers. They seemed to be all over lately, gathering up kids.

"If there's room, grab up three more."

London hoped the soldier didn't mean him, but just in case, he ducked behind a barrel and crept along the ground, using more barrels and giant crates as cover.

It would be awful to get captured now. London had spent years avoiding being sent to a workhouse, a fate that was the usual choice for orphans these days. The crown had replaced schools with workhouses, arguing that the children of *good* families had at-home learning and the ones who couldn't learn at home ought to be put to work as soon as possible, since it was their future.

It was nonsense.

His mum had been a teacher, but there was no work for teachers once there were no more city schools. The crown simply hadn't cared about teachers—or kids—for years.

London thought back to that day his mother had been shoved onto the ship.

Run, love. Run and hide.

Mum!

Go on. I'll find you. Only take what you need. I'll find you someday, she said, shoving him toward a pile of cargo and running.

He heard her cry. He saw them capture her.

That was five years ago, and London still came to the docks, hoping she'd be here one of these days. He watched ships carry away other moms and dads, big brothers and sisters, too. He'd looked at a lot of faces, and never saw any of them come back.

"No one comes back," he muttered.

His footsteps sounded too loud as he slipped between crates to try to find the passenger ship that would take him to Northland City. He'd been eyeing the sailing options for weeks, and finally there was one leaving today.

He stopped at the bottom of the walkway and noticed a girl about his age shimmying up a tall pole—or whatever the thing that held the sails was called. This ship appeared to be a cargo vessel, though. No cabins for passengers here!

"You, lad!" shouted a tall, bony fellow. "You one of the new ones?"

What if he slipped on board *this* ship and saved the money he was planning to spend on a ticket?

"I am," London said, deciding quickly that it was best to get on this ship while officers were circling. In the distance he could see the one who'd been pursuing him.

"Help get these crates on board, and then you can go get settled into quarters," the older boy said.

London grabbed one of the largest crates and lifted. "Lead the way."

"Save a bit of energy in case there's no wind and we need to row!" The boy smiled and grabbed another wooden box.

London laughed and shared a joke of his own. "Nah. Get it all on the ship so we can have a kip."

The boy paused. "A *kip*? You a Northlander, then?"

"Heading home," London said, which was sort of true. He did intend to make Northland his home.

They loaded the rest of the cargo, and then, as they were walking away from the cargo hold, the other boy said, "Be sure to check in with Tanner if you haven't already, Northy."

When they separated, London headed back to the ship's cargo area and squeezed into a space he'd left between crates, pulled a tarp down, and went to sleep under it. He hadn't had a chance to buy any food, but he'd find food in the hold. He patted the bag of money deep in his pocket—stowing away on the ship meant it was *all* still there.

The thought of the gold he carried gave him a momentary twinge. *No one* took gold to sea. It was bad luck. That's why London had only enough gold coins to buy his ticket, and the rest of his savings was in silver, copper, and jewels.

He debated tossing the gold overboard.

Wasn't it just a superstition, though? What danger could there possibly be in carrying gold to sea? The only things in the sea—other than fish—were kelpies, and if the water horses cared about gold, they'd bother the nobs walking along the canals in Glass City.

London wasn't going to let superstition steal his money. He kept his gold coins.

CHAPTER 2

◆——◆——◆

Otter

Ottilie Jo Maul wasn't sure she'd ever feel right on land. Her family and friends called her Otter, since she was only at home in or on water. Her fathers claimed they used to have to tether her to her family's ship, the H.M.S. *Tempest*, to keep her from leaping overboard.

Today, though, she was on land, which had the peculiar tendency to *not* sway like the deck of her ship. She wasn't good at being on a surface that didn't move.

Glass City wasn't the absolute *worst* place. The canals, at least, stretched along the streets. Within them were dark waters that would work like roads if one sailed inland. No one was allowed to do so in the royal city, though. Boats must dock. Sailors must walk on land.

It was absurd. That's what it was.

"Sick already, lass?" Her father glanced at her, worry in his eyes.

Captain Maul looked too big for the narrow city streets. Although if you asked Otter, he was as polished as the finest man in the royal court—but not as mean. On Otter's last visit to land, she'd spewed her lunch all over the shoes of a man at court and gotten no sympathy.

Hopefully, there would be no vomiting this visit!

"Not too bad," Otter hedged.

"Glad your stomach's cooperating. Got to keep all your vittles inside!" As Captain Maul nodded, his enormous beard made a soft clattering sound. He kept his beard braided, and each braid ended with tiny beads or clips. Otter had liked the effect so much that she copied it on her own multihued hair; she had also woven in bits of shells and sparkling stones.

"*Yes*, but I belong on the ship," Otter grumbled, trying not to wince from the dizzy way she always felt when the land wasn't moving.

"Ottilie Jo Maul."

She glanced at him.

"Do you *need* to go back to the ship?"

She sighed. "Da . . ."

"You *said* you could do it this time," he reminded her. Gruff as he was, he sounded worried. "Do you need help?"

Otter looked away. "I was hoping I could do without."

Her father unslung a bag from his shoulder, and from within it, he pulled a cloak. When he settled it around her shoulders, she breathed a sigh of relief. Only one material countered her land sickness: dragon hide.

Most people didn't even know dragons existed, and the Glass Queen was determined to keep it that way. The H.M.S. *Tempest* was the only vessel that sought them out, sailing into seas that Her Majesty had declared unnavigable in order to keep all other ships out. And to make their cover story work, the *Tempest* also carried cargo to the north for the queen. In that regard, they functioned like any other ship. It was the cargo they brought home that made all the difference.

Only the captain and crew had the queen's papers to sail the Crimson Sea, and only the H.M.S. *Tempest* could collect dragon hide.

Sometimes Otter wondered about how easily the queen lied, but these lies kept the dragons safe. Otter would feel worse if people hunted the dragons.

Captain Maul and his crew were the only ones who knew the truth—the Crimson Sea *could* be treacherous, not because of rocks or currents, but because of thrashing dragons. This was a risk they took, though, to carry some of the most valuable cargo in the Glass Empire. Dragon skin, the layer they shed, was the stuff the queen needed for her guards' armor and it was the stuff that every gown the queen wore contained. It was impervious to fire, difficult to pierce, and water repelling. Every member of the crew of the *Tempest* also got a set of skins to wear as a cloak or an underlayer. Besides the Queen's Ravens, they were the only ones allowed to wear it.

If they sold the skin, they'd be wealthy—or maybe dead. Crossing the Glass Queen sounded terribly dangerous, even though she'd *seemed* nice enough when Otter first met her. Although their actual meeting was cut short on account of Otter's sick stomach, the queen didn't seem upset.

And she'd invited Otter back.

Otter and her father walked in silence toward the Glass Castle, and as Otter looked up at the towers piercing the sky, she found it hard to understand how anyone could like a building so tall that flying buttresses were essential to keep the structure from collapsing. Living in a place like the castle meant being far from the ground, and that was way too far from the water.

When they arrived, the captain told a guard, "The Glass Queen is expecting us."

The Raven nodded. Every Raven knew that the H.M.S. *Tempest* sailed to the reaches of the map in order to bring that "fabric" back. Even when it was dyed black, it kept the iridescence of dragons, so their armor looked like the sheen of raven feathers.

"Captain Maul." The Raven nodded. "Little Maul."

Otter rolled her eyes. "It's *Otter*, if you please."

Before entering the castle, Otter's father held out a hand.

Silently, she gave him her cloak. They didn't want to draw attention to the fact that she had a cloak made of the same fabric as the armor that the Ravens wore. The Ravens knew the secret of the dragon hide, but not everyone in the castle was a Raven, so it was best to avoid wearing dragon skin within Glass City lest there be awkward questions.

They followed the guard into the castle—and up staircase after staircase until they were on the topmost floor of the highest tower of the castle.

The Raven ushered them into a room, and they were suddenly alone with the queen—well, as alone as the queen ever was. There was still one guard at the door in a high tower in the Glass Castle. Other guards kept every door and passage to the castle secure.

The queen smiled at them. "Nice to see you brought the child, Captain Maul."

Her father shrugged. "Someday, she'll be the one you need to deal with, Your Ladyship, so she needs to get used to you. I get older every time I turn around."

"Indeed." The queen looked at Otter as she spoke to her father. "Have you considered sending her to Corvus until she needs to take over the ship? My heir attends the school."

"Ottilie doesn't like being away from the sea, Your Lady."

The queen sighed loudly. "Your *Majesty*, Captain. The proper address in my empire is 'Your Majesty.'"

"Sorry, Your Majesty. My daughter is happiest at sea. Same as me. Seawater in our veins, don't you know?"

"Scientifically impossible, Captain Maul." The Glass Queen had a smile that looked surprisingly friendly now. For all that people whispered she was icy and heartless, she'd only ever spoken kindly to Otter. Now she turned to Otter and asked, "So how are you feeling on the land this time?"

"I'm doing my best, Your Majesty," Otter said. "Doesn't make sense how it stays still."

"I see. And if the land were to move . . ."

"It would help," Otter managed to say.

She was trying hard not to show her discomfort. Being up in a stone tower this far from the sea wasn't doing great things for her stomach. She closed her eyes and thought watery thoughts of sea, salt, wind. She imagined swaying over the water, watching for dragons. For a moment, she could taste the brine in the air.

Wings brushed her cheeks, and Otter opened her eyes to

see the tail end of what looked like an entire flock of dragonets being chased out of the room by a gargoyle.

The queen's voice sounded far away as she asked, "What *is* she?"

"Ottilie is my *daughter*, Your Majesty." He handed Otter his bag, which held her cloak.

She slid her hand inside and touched the dragon hide—and the twisting in her belly eased. Touching that magical stuff made her land sickness settle briefly, same as if she touched the sea.

The queen looked concerned. "Perhaps my alchemist can create a tincture to ease your discomfort on land, Ottilie. He asked for challenges of the nonlethal sort recently."

The Glass Queen motioned to the Raven at the door. When her guard stepped closer, the queen ordered, "Send for Nightshade. I will meet with him when these guests leave."

Once the Raven was gone, Otter felt her father's heavy hand pat her back, pushing her closer to the queen.

"You must take care, Captain Maul," the queen said softly. "My Ravens tell me that there are plots to invade your hunting ground and steal your cargo. I *need* those plots to be thwarted."

"But how can they invade?" Otter blurted out. "No one knows what we harvest. And the *Tempest* is the fastest ship in the empire!"

Otter didn't mention that they were fast because they followed dragons—which let the ship find the best currents. They *also* caught just enough fish for the crew, thanks to dragons.

"We have a traitor," the queen announced.

"Your Majesty"—Captain Maul cleared his throat—"Ottilie is right. No one else could sail where we do. The seas there—"

"Yes, yes, I know. Maelstroms. Shallows. No one can cross the great whirlpool to the Crimson Sea." The queen continued to speak softly, despite their apparent privacy. "I am aware. But greed erases logic sometimes, and my betrayer knows what precious cargo you gather."

Greed would have to be awfully powerful to send anyone else to the part of the sea where the H.M.S. *Tempest* sailed. The whirlpools, for it wasn't just one, were immense. They churned the sea in a froth, and sometimes Otter doubted that the *Tempest* would stay above water.

"I am also aware that you have an understanding with the things under the water that might otherwise add dangers to those storms and whirlpools," the queen added in a whisper.

Otter nodded. It was more than an "understanding" with the dragons—it was love, awe, and respect.

During a few storms, dragons had even nudged the ship to safety.

The queen looked to the gargoyle that was perched on the ledge of the tower window before she withdrew a parchment from her robes. It had the royal seal impressed upon it in deep-blue wax. "No one else knows what you do for me, Captain. It must always stay that way."

The papers were the annual decree that the H.M.S. *Tempest* was a royally sanctioned vessel. Boarding or attacking the ship was an assault on the Glass Queen herself. No other ship had such a status, and Otter had never seen the paper before.

"I won't tell," Otter swore. "Because they . . . the dragons deserve . . ."

"You regard the dragons with favor?" the Glass Queen asked.

"Yes! We are alive only because they allow it. They could sink us if they chose," Otter said.

"And yet you seek the sea," the queen said.

Otter and her father exchanged a look. There was no way to explain it, not to landfolk. Being out in the sea on a still day—no land in sight—was pure peace. And when the wind rose to fill sails, sliding the ship across the water, it was a marvel.

"She's magic," her father said, glancing at Otter.

"That explains many things," the queen murmured.

Otter nodded. They *were* talking about the sea, right?

"You would be an asset to my Ravens," the queen continued, "but I am happy that you are out there protecting our precious cargo."

"We will do everything in our power to make sure the *Tempest* is safe," the captain said. "We're just finishing up loading the outgoing cargo for the trip north. We'll be careful—"

"And if anything does happen, we'll dump our *other* cargo before it goes to your enemies!" Otter declared.

"Sail safely," the queen said.

Then she held out a second parchment toward Captain Maul. This one was sealed with black wax. "If I should perish before you return," she said, "these are the people you must tell of your inbound cargo."

He bowed deeply. "Your Majesty. We shall not fail you."

"You never do, Maul." The Glass Queen looked at Otter and said, "It is an honor to speak with you, Ottilie."

Then, in a blink, they were dismissed.

Her father said nothing until they were boarding the *Tempest*. Then he put his arm around her shoulders. "I think *you* are the best magic I've seen, Ottilie. Tan and I would be lost without you."

"Same. I'm lucky to have such good dads."

"Right you are. Now, go on with you. We have work to do. Seas to sail. Pirates to avoid."

"Yes, sir, Captain," she said, grinning. She might be worried about the things the queen had said, but all that mattered now was that the *Tempest* was setting sail.

Otter would be where she belonged again—at sea.

CHAPTER 3

◆──◆──◆

Sofia

Life in the streets of Glass City wasn't as awful as a lot of things. Jail was worse. Workhouses were worse. Being sent off on one of the "relocation" ships was *far* worse.

Most of the kids who became thieves—like Sofia—were on the streets because their parents had been shipped off. But now something new was happening at the docks: suddenly, there were new ships, and they were collecting kids.

"What are they doing?" asked Alexandria, one of the younger thieves, who was tucked behind Sofia.

"Stealing humans. You shouldn't be out here right now," Sofia said, gently pushing Alex toward their home. "Go through the closest entrance, toward the tunnel."

"So—"

"Go." Sofia looked back to the dock. New wasn't good, not *this* kind of new.

"Vermin! That's what you thieves are," a man yelled at a boy he'd knocked to the ground by the ship.

Sofia watched as several men in masks rounded up about

six boys. People on the dock looked away. She wanted to help, but she was one girl. What could she do?

When one of the masked men glanced away, the smallest boy took off. The man reached for him, but an enormous beaked gargoyle swooped down and knocked the man onto his bum.

Sofia stepped out of her hiding place. She held out a hand to the boy while the gargoyle hovered in the air behind him, like a stone shield.

"Come on," Sofia said, and as soon as the boy's hand was in hers, she ran with him till they reached two narrow stones that they slipped between. There were other entrances to the underground, but Sofia liked this one best because no adult could fit through it.

Sofia could feel the boy shaking as she led him by the hand through the dark tunnel into the underground—the part of the city *under* Glass City.

"It's okay. You're okay," she told the boy as he hesitated. "Slide your foot forward, step, slide. Soon it'll be light again."

In a few minutes they were in the cavernous underground city. Years ago, when the water levels had risen, most of Glass City had been rebuilt on top of the old city. Entire buildings and roads were down here, old shops and courtyards, and the street kids claimed the city as their own. Sure, it flooded sometimes, but there were plenty of dry areas for groups of kids to settle in.

Sofia stopped when they arrived at the vine-covered wall that hid one of the doors to enter her home—the House of Florence.

Someday she hoped there would be a House of Sofia. She wanted to do what Florie had done: help the kids like them, kids who needed a family. They worked, lived, and ate together. The House of Florence was just like a real family, except they were all kids.

Tonight, Sofia was late getting back, and she knew Florie would worry. She hoped they hadn't sent anyone to look for her! But if she hadn't been late, this boy would have been shoved onto a ship and sent to . . . somewhere.

"Do you know where they were going to take you?" she asked.

"That man said we was kelpie food. Too many 'vermin,' he said, like people are *rats*. So . . . I guess the ship was carrying us out to sea so they could dump us. I'd rather not get eaten, so I tried to get away." The boy looked around. "What happens now?"

Before Sofia could answer, Florie saw her with the new child and motioned her forward. "Who is this?"

"Orphan," she said. "They were trying to snatch him and a bunch of kids for one of those new ships."

"How many kids did they catch this time?" Florie sounded angry.

"Six I know of." The boy looked like he was going to cry. "I was only at the docks because I watched them load up my pap there the other day. Came back there because . . ." He shrugged. "It was stupid. I just missed him. That was the last place I saw him, and . . ."

Sofia reached out and hugged him briefly. "Not stupid."

"Something needs to be done!" Florie said. "They've closed

schools, stolen parents, and now *this*? We've given the queen plenty of time to live up to her new promises! Her gifts of food are useful, but it's not *enough* change!"

"A gargoyle saved him," Sofia explained. "Maybe a bunch of us could help, too? I could see if someone down here can talk to gargoyles or . . . ?"

"Sure. It's a start." Florie nodded, and she knew his mind was occupied thinking up some sort of plan. Whatever it was, she would help. Sometimes she thought that the news they brought him was as important as the things they stole. Florie never went to Glass City because kids in modified medical assistance chairs—especially ones with extra-large wheels— stood out.

The first rule of thieves was to avoid notice.

When Florie finally met her eyes, he said, "We'll set up rescue groups and try to work with the gargoyles, too." He paused and frowned. "But I'll have another job for you, Sofia, that I'll tell you about later. Something no one else here *could* do."

Something about those words made her shiver. It could just be that he wasn't telling her now because the new boy was with them, but somehow, she thought it was more than that.

"Whatever the house needs," Sofia said—and she meant it with her whole heart. The thieves had saved her, and she wanted to save them right back. Any way she could. As often as she could. That's what a real family was.

Then Florie turned to the boy. "And you. We all chose new names to start a new life here. In every house is a group of names, so thieves know where you belong just by hearing your name."

Once the boy nodded, Florie started reading a list of names.

The boy interrupted a minute or so into the list Florie read. "Rio," he said. "I like that one. I'm called Rio now."

"Rio it is! Sofia can take you over to the food and introduce you around. Then tomorrow you can start earning your keep. While you're here, you'll learn, help with food, or teach the little ones if you can read. When you're ready, you'll steal for us. Food isn't free . . . at least not usually. The queen's been sending some, but it's never enough for this many mouths."

"Makes sense." Rio paused and looked at Sofia. "You saved my life, you know? I don't know if they were for real going to feed me to the kelpies, but whatever it was they was doing, it wasn't nice."

Florie said nothing, simply turned his chair around, and left.

"Come on," Sofia urged, tugging Rio's arm. "Food. Then we'll figure out where you'll sleep."

"Why are you helping me?"

Sofia shrugged. "Someone helped me. I helped you. Someday you'll help someone else. It's how it works. A lot of adults seem to have forgotten that."

"They're not all bad," Rio objected.

Maybe he was right, but "not all bad" wasn't the same as good.

Sofia showed Rio where the food was stored. "We only eat our fill. And at meals, the littlest eat first." She handed him a chunk of bread and an apple.

Then she led him to the clothing bins. The clothes were washed as clean as they could be. This part of the underground—the part where the House of Florence made their home—had barrels where they gathered the water that leaked from the pipes under the city.

She pointed at the clothes, divided by size. "These are the extras for new kids. Clean. No bugs. Just take two sets."

Then she walked toward a group of boys and introduced them to Rio. "Florie says he's allowed to stay, so can he sleep near one of you or your groups?"

There was silence till a boy named Rotterdam finally answered, "I'll take him."

Rott was the one who had brought her to Florie, and as far as the underground went, there weren't many people more trustworthy than him.

"Come with me, Rio," Rott said. "I'll show you where you'll sleep, and then bring you back to Sof."

As the boys walked away, Sofia sighed. Everything here worked. They'd found a way, and it was due to Florie.

The House of Florence was, in her opinion, the best thieves' house in Glass City. But it was starting to get crowded in the underground. All the various thief houses were getting fuller as more kids ended up out on the streets. At least each house had its own area that was sort of like a small village, entered by its own hidden doors and tunnels.

Sofia hoped life in the Glass City would get better again, and the food piles left by the Queen's Ravens were a start, but the kids needed more—things like heat and clean water would be nice. And they needed ideas for what to do with their futures. Kids grew up, and without any schools, what would they do when they were older?

For now, they worked, and they learned on the street or underground. They shared their food and space. At the end of the day, they presented their hauls to Florie. They trusted *him*, not some queen who had been part of making the problems in the first place.

What they had underground wasn't perfect, but life in the House of Florence was a lot better than starving aboveground—or being fed to kelpies.

CHAPTER 4

◆———◆———◆

London

No one had warned London that being at sea would feel like this. The ship lifted, twisted, and crashed. London's stomach followed it. He felt like he was being tossed around like a pickpocket's treasure.

And he had no one to blame. It had been his own fool idea to stow away with the cargo instead of buying a ticket and securing a bunk. London had thought it was a fine plan. He was saving money, and he was used to scrounging food. He'd lived on the streets for five years. How hard could this be? London had found a space in the very lowest belly of the boat, under the crew's quarters, and he'd been happy with his decision—right up until the ship hit a storm the second day at sea.

He'd seen waves batter the docks, and he'd seen rain heavy enough to flood the canals in Glass City and make it rain in the underground. Nothing he'd even *imagined* had prepared him for a storm at sea. London felt like he was heaving everything he'd ever eaten in his life. Clutching his angry stomach, he was crouched under a slick-skinned tarp, tucked between lashed-down barrels, while the ship tilted over so far that things flew around the belly of the ship. Getting squished by cargo between bouts of vomiting wasn't how he'd planned to spend his first week at sea!

Eventually, he must've slept, because the next thing he knew, someone was kicking him gently. He opened his eyes to a girl who looked to be about his age.

She nudged him with her boot. "No pirate's life for you, eh?"

His first thought was that she would be useless as a thief with her thick multicolored hair and loud voice. Seashells clattered as she moved. Absolutely nothing about her blended into the background.

He scrambled to his feet and tried to stand, but the boat was still rocking.

He made a noise, definitely *not* a whimper. Just a noise.

"You'll be fine, yeah? Storm's passing," she said, holding out a hand. "Or maybe we passed out of it. Hard to say from down here. Rain let up, though."

She curled her fingers in a "come on" gesture, and London grabbed her hand. He was starting to think he might not be able to walk any other way.

"You can't *fight* the sea," she said, holding on to him tightly. "Think of it like a horse, yeah? You let your body become a part of the beast. Just roll through the bumps with it."

The image of becoming half horse made him laugh—and think of the Netherwhere. There he'd seen the sort of creatures that made him think any kind of strange was possible.

"I'm London," he managed as he swayed with the ship.

"Ottilie, but the crew just calls me Otter."

"Are you a passenger?" London asked, although he was pretty sure cargo ships didn't take passengers.

Otter laughed. "Every single trip, I am a passenger." She tugged him forward. "Let's get you up to the captain."

London jerked away. "Can't. I, er, didn't exactly *buy* a ticket, so—"

Otter caught his wrist. "I know. I'll tell my dad you're my friend. He'll find you a job on ship until we dock." She scrunched up her nose. "Maybe dip you in the sea first. You smell bad."

"Your dad?"

"Captain Otto Maul," Otter said, standing taller as she spoke. "I'm named after him, but most of the crew calls *him* Captain Maul."

London swallowed hard again, but this time it was fear he was holding back. Captain Maul? With a name like that, the captain sounded scary, and confessing to a person like *that* seemed different than confessing to someone like the very forgetful Master Nightshade, who had been the only adult London had more or less had to obey, and only for the short time he'd worked for the alchemist.

"Maybe you could pretend you didn't see me," London suggested.

Otter laughed. "Nah, someone is sure to smell you." She made a face and pushed him toward the ladder. "Up we go."

London didn't see another option. He couldn't exactly hide now that someone knew he was here. Unlike the alleys of Glass City, a ship—even one as big as the H.M.S. *Tempest*—was a hard place to vanish.

He climbed up to the storage level, past the crew's quarters, and then stood on the top deck trying to get his feet under him.

After one deep breath, London followed Otter along the deck, dragging his feet and trying to come up with an answer that didn't involve being tossed overboard like a snack for the kelpies or whatever other beasts roamed the seas.

Up there, people were scanning the sea on every side. One person, a tall man with a braided beard that flapped in the wind like a bunch of serpents, stared at Otter when they walked toward him.

"Da—" Otter started.

"Ottilie Jo Maul, did you bring another cargo rat after I said not to?" The man folded his arms over his barrel-sized chest. "We talked about this, child. You can't just collect street urchins and think I'll give them berth and bread."

Instead of giving him up, Otter pouted as if she *had* stowed him away. She stared at the giant man and said, "I get *lonely*, Da. I need friends. They need food."

He looked at London before glancing back at Otter and saying, "Do you think the queen wants us bringing people out here?"

Otter shrugged. "Probably not."

"We don't travel where the passenger ships go," he told them both. "There are rules. She could pull our papers, and then where would we be?"

"Da . . ." She motioned at London. "He's harmless. Look at him!"

London tried his best to focus on Otter and the captain, but now that he was standing on deck, he saw the sea. The water was everywhere, rolling in every direction, glittering like the sun had dripped gems all over it. He'd never imagined anything so big. He hadn't known how vast it was from inside the cargo hold.

The sliver of the sea he'd seen before this trip was only the bit visible from the docks. Out here it was different. Nothing but water as far as he could see in every direction! Waves rose up, and he found that he was watching for kelpies.

Hoping for *kelpies*, who did that?

"Does it ever end?" he asked, not meaning to say it aloud.

The captain and Otter both paused in whatever else they'd been saying. The captain grinned. "Only when land gets in the way, but we work around that."

"What my dad means is that there's water everywhere. We scuttled our way inland through a few channels even." Otter looked proud, as if there was some honor in cutting through land in a boat.

"This boat fits in the canals?" he asked. Maybe it was a magic boat . . . ?

"No, lad, channels are something like a canal, but they're best thought of like bits of the sea that decided to push into the land so as we can connect to the next bit of open sea."

London nodded, trying to picture it.

Then the captain's hand came down on London's shoulder. "So, you fancy her?"

"Your *daughter*? No, sir. I mean, she's fine and all, but—"

"The sea, lad. You fancy the sea?" The captain laughed. "I've seen that look you're wearing. See it in my own looking glass often enough, as a matter of fact."

"It's incredible." London stared back out at the water. "I feel like I could go just about anywhere, and I *want to*."

Otter whispered to her dad, "See? Not a land rat! So, he can stay?"

Captain Maul nodded. "That he can." He paused. "Best be telling him what we're doing, though, and keep him in the fresh air a bit. He looks green around the gills."

"You're carrying cargo to Northland," London said, standing straighter in pride for knowing the answer. "I was going to settle there to start over, and there was a thief snatcher on the dock, so I . . . I mean, not that I'm a *thief*, Captain Maul."

The captain stared at him. "Oh?"

London took a look at the captain, massive but seemingly kind, and decided to tell the truth. "Fine. I *was* a thief, but what can a kid do? Need to eat, and there are lots of us—"

"Did someone *send* you here?" Captain Maul no longer looked kind. It was as if he was swelling in size, becoming scarier by the moment. "Were you to signal someone?"

"No!"

The captain and Otter exchanged a glance, but they didn't speak.

London stressed, "On my life, I swear! I was running, and one of your crew thought I was meant to be here, and"—he shrugged—"you were headed where I was going. Free ride? Safe from the snatcher? I'm not a fool. I came on board. Hauled a bunch of boxes, too, and I'll work while I'm here."

"I think he's honest, Da," Otter murmured.

All Captain Maul said was, "There's a water basin in my quarters. Let the boy wash up. He can join us at repast."

"Repast?" London echoed.

"Food," Otter clarified. "Wash. Feed." She paused and then grinned widely. "Da, you got me a pet!"

"A *pet*?" London stared at her. A moment ago, he'd been worrying that the captain was going to throw him overboard. Now he was just worrying that they were a little bonkers.

The captain rolled his eyes, but he looked less likely to toss anyone in the sea as he chuckled.

Otter started laughing. "You should see your face, London! Come on."

He took one last long look at the waves, not really wanting to go into a room but suddenly glad he'd picked *this* boat with these people.

He followed Otter, but he kept glancing at the sea. There was something magical about the endless roll of water. It glinted like the gems on every nob's wrist or neck, but it wasn't jewels. Just water—and somehow this water looked better than anything he'd seen in Glass City.

CHAPTER 5

◆——◆——◆

Otter

Otter had started to lead London toward the captain's chambers when she felt a familiar itch all over her body. "Not now!" she muttered. "This can't be happening *now*."

Only one thing made her skin itch like that: dragons. Otter felt the creature surging to the surface, felt scales and skin. The creature's mind connected to hers. That had happened as long as she was alive, or as long as she remembered.

And in that connection, Otter felt a part of herself want to stretch and dive. She couldn't go into the sea anymore. In fact, for reasons she didn't understand, her fathers were insistent she stay out of the sea.

Still, she often had dreams that almost felt like memories where she was swimming alongside giant scaled creatures. Dragons. All around her were the iridescent flickers of dragon scales.

Foolish, lovely dreams!

But now, in this moment, it felt like this dragon was calling to her, even though it was silent.

"We're not your enemy!" Otter thought-spoke toward the dragon. "Friends!"

There was no reply—as the dragons never *spoke* back to her—but Otter got an image in her head of the size of this unfamiliar dragon who was racing toward the ship.

None had ever been this big. It could capsize them.

"Are *you* sick?" London asked, pausing and touching her arm lightly. "You look like I felt."

"No! But you need a tether so you don't wash overboard!" She looked around to see who was near. Loud as she could, she yelled, "Incoming!"

"Incoming? What?" London gaped at her.

"Can't explain. Danger." Otter looked around for a tether. Where was the blasted tether? Finally, she saw one and dragged him to it.

She slung a vest at London. "Put this on! Hurry."

All around them, the voices of the crew rose.

"Incoming!"

"Otter called!"

"Tethers, man!"

The ship started to rise up.

"What—"

"Trust me, London." She hooked a tether to his vest that would chain him to the ship's deck. Then she tethered herself to a longer chain. "Do not take your vest off, no matter what!"

The ship lurched again from the rush of water. The creature was surging upward, breaching as if the ship wasn't even there. The last time they'd had a direct breach, it had been worse than the biggest storm of the season.

"Otter!" Her other father, Tanner, the *Tempest*'s first mate, slid toward her as if he had no fear of falling. "What can you tell me?"

"Too far from the Crimson Sea, but it's a dragon . . . Tell Da it's enormous," she told Tanner. "We need to steer away. And get yourself lashed."

Tanner gave her a look as if to remind her that he was the parent here, but *he* couldn't feel how big this dragon was.

"Stay here," she ordered London, unspooling more of the line that tethered her to the ship. "Whatever you see, whatever you hear, stay hooked onto the ship, yeah?"

As soon as he nodded, Otter slid across the deck toward Tanner, who had a tether now and was standing at the captain's side. Their speed in getting there was aided by the next tilt of the ship.

The captain's beard braids were flapping wildly. He pointed to a dark-green shape under the waves. "Look at her."

"She's huge, Da!" Otter stared downward as a mammoth clawed foot broke the sea's surface and kicked. She could see bits of the net twisted around the dragon's foot.

"And far too close to the ship," the captain said, sounding alarmed.

"She's caught!" Otter yelled. "Tangled in the nets. Curling . . . Da! She's *curling* into the nets."

The beast was caught in the nets the crew used to skim the shed skin out of the sea. The nets were vast and had holes big enough for fish or other small creatures to escape, but not a dragon!

"Let loose the nets, or we'll be pulled under when she dives," the captain yelled.

The sheer size of the foot that smacked the side of the ship seemed impossible. It was like an oversized anchor—and twice as dangerous.

"She's bigger than the ship, Da. Largest. One. *Ever!*" Otter yelled, batting her hair out of her face.

"Please," she thought-whispered to the creature. "Please don't sink us."

But another one of the dragon's claws raked the side of the *Tempest*. The sound of breaking wood—a sound that every sailor feared—was devastating.

The ship started to tilt madly as the dragon tried to escape from the net.

"Faster, lads! Cut those nets free faster!" the captain yelled.

Like every other crew member, Otter drew her sword, using the blade to hack at the rope nearest her. "Please don't sink us. We're not trying to catch you," Otter thought-spoke. "We're cutting the net loose."

Another wave washed over the deck as the beast flailed and twisted.

"Bilges!" Tanner called. "Keep pumping out all this water!"

Finally, the creature's tail broke the surface, lashing out of the sea toward the deck.

"Holy mother of pearls, Captain," Tanner whispered as

the barbs on the tip of the dragon's tail shredded one of the *Tempest*'s spanker sails.

Gears creaked loudly as the crew loosened the nets and more of the ropes broke. Finally, the ship righted herself with a splash as the dragon was freed.

Otter concentrated on sending her thoughts to the beast as it left: "We meant you no harm."

To the crew, Otter said, "She's gone. She's left."

"Both bilges still working," one of the crew called. "Still taking on water but pumping steady."

Otter exhaled, thankful for the good news.

"Did we save any nets?" her dad asked.

One of the men shook his head. "Total loss."

"The rear railing is shattered, too," another crew member added.

"Push it overboard." The captain looked around. "Assess the provisions needed to reach Coventry. Toss the rest."

"Captain—"

"Do it or lighten our weight by adding yourself to the list to go overboard." The captain met his unhappy expression steadily, then turned away to get another damage report.

"Hull has a leak, but not bad," another man pronounced. "Crack. The boys and me patched it on the inside with a swath of dra—with *our special cargo*."

While the crew was assessing the damage, Otter made her way to the remains of the mizzenmast. Between the hole in the side and the broken mast, the ship was going to need a few weeks of repairs before she could sail again—that was if they could even make it to shore. The ship was listing on its side, and Otter heard someone suggest discarding the cargo. If they tossed the cargo, her dads would have no way to pay for repairs.

Freedom was expensive.

"Is that sail salvageable?"

"Aye, Miss Otter," one of the older men said. He gestured above her head. "Top of the mizzenmast is a loss, though. We can save the sails, but the mast will need to be replaced when we reach land."

"Do you need help?" London asked from behind her.

She wasn't sure when he'd joined them, but he looked strangely calm. Maybe he hadn't realized it was a—

"Haven't seen a dragon that big before," London said. "Didn't even know they were out here."

Otter had no words, so she just started to climb. *No one* was to know dragons were real, and she hadn't had a chance to tell London about the *Tempest*'s mission yet. The big lizard-like creatures weren't seen outside the Crimson Sea often enough for anyone to think the "sea dragon sightings" were anything more than herds of kelpies spotted by sailors with poor eyesight. Dragons? Most people laughed at the thought—at least those who lived on land did.

By the time Otter was halfway up the mast, she realized that London had shimmied up after her. He followed as she ascended to where the wood had splintered.

Otter tied a rope that had been fastened to the shredded sail around her waist and wrapped it securely over a leg, too.

"Ottilie Jo Maul!" Tanner called from on deck below her. He

rarely used her full name like that. Tanner often claimed that the captain did so often enough for both of her fathers.

She waved at him and then muttered, "My dads worry, but I can climb—and if I fall, I swim better than anyone on the ship. So there!"

Down below, she heard Tanner ordering the crew back to work.

"We're trying to knock the broken part down, right?" London asked.

"If we don't, it'll crack and fall on someone—or tear the other sails. It has to go."

"Makes sense," London said.

"I'm going to kick this wood until it shatters. Pieces will fall on us. We're likely to get a few scrapes."

"Obviously." He was grinning widely, as if he was enjoying almost being sunk by a dragon and now risking splinters big enough to use to stir a stewpot.

"You're not frightened?" she asked.

"Nah!"

Otter wasn't going to argue that he ought to be. She didn't have the arm strength to push the mast down alone, and most of the other crew members were too heavy to get up this high safely. London's willingness to help would make this not only possible, but *easier.*

"Ottilie! I swear to Nicholas you're going to make me lose the rest of my hair." Her father's voice carried across the ship, and in that instant, she realized that more than a few of the crewmen were watching her and the captain both.

"That's Northy!" one of the men called, pointing at London.

41

"I'm like to throttle the both of you if you don't come down from there," Tanner added.

Great. Now *both* dads were scowling at her.

"Are they going to toss me overboard?" London asked.

"No." Otter hoped she was telling the truth. Her dads looked angry.

"This is easy as pie," she called back to the crew and her dads.

Bracing herself, Otter started kicking the already cracked wood. Pieces of it rained down as she made progress.

"Hold on to me in case I fall," she told London, because she wasn't sure she could keep clinging to the mast and not fall.

Good to have someone brace me, she thought, extra grateful that there was another kid on board.

As she kicked, she also thought about the possibility of her family being stuck on shore. Corsets and dresses. No dragons. Boring. She thought, too, about the queen's warning of pirates and attacks.

And at each thought, her feet hammered at the wood until it gave a thundering crack and fell away.

Cheers rang out as the topmost piece of wood detached from the mast and crashed to the deck. The sails were safe.

Underneath them, the crew heaved the piece of mast overboard, and Otter looked around at the sails. A few stitches and patches wouldn't go amiss, but if she hadn't dislodged that wobbly bit of the broken mast, the sails would've been shredded.

She swung out from the mast like an acrobat and let out

a victory "whoop!" Her hair came unbound, and the wind whipped it around like tentacles streaming from her head. It was such a glorious feeling to be free! Alive! At sea!

"Otter!" London reached for her as she swung out of arm's reach.

Dangling upside down over the deck, Otter caught sight of her father climbing up the mast. He looked like he'd just seen a goat dance by dressed in his best knickers.

"The captain is going to toss me overboard," London muttered. "A watery death . . ."

"Can you swim?" she teased.

"Kelpies. Dragons." London stared at the sea. "No land in sight. I'm *doomed!*"

"Welcome to the *Tempest*," Otter said, laughing. "It's never dull around here!"

The captain was just under them. "Get down before you fall, both of you. If one of them beasts surfaced while you're up here dangling—"

"I'd *know.*" Otter sighed as she started to work her way free of the ropes. "I'd feel them, Da. That one was just faster than most. Usually we have more notice, yeah? I'm safe. Tan's safe. Crew's safe. The *Tempie* needs a little patching, though."

"That she does." The captain patted the mast as if the ship could feel him. Then he looked down to the deck. Every person aboard was dripping wet. "Least everyone smells better."

The kids dropped the rest of the way down, and Otter got a quick hug from the captain.

"She's fine," the captain said to her other dad, who still

looked like he was about to have a fit. The captain opened his arm in an invitation to Tanner.

Tanner's arms went around him, and they hugged tightly, murmuring words of love.

And Otter braced herself. It was perfectly normal for a kid to have parents, but sometimes land folk were particular about her having two dads. London didn't seem to notice, but Otter was still waiting.

"Our daughter is going to be the death of me," Tanner said.

"Let's feed her—and you," her other dad said. "You'll both feel better."

London's eyes lit up. "I haven't eaten in a day and half. Food sounds good to me if I'm still welcome . . ."

And Otter let out a sigh of relief. Her new friend was fine after all. She smiled and said, "Sure, and you can tell us why you weren't surprised to see what you *thought* was a dragon, yeah?"

CHAPTER 6

◆———◆———◆

London

After a quick glance at the water, London followed them toward the captain's quarters for a bite to eat and, hopefully, a few answers. A storm *and* a dragon? Today was a lot more interesting than whole months in Glass City. The only times he'd had such adventures were in the Netherwhere. He sighed. He'd really *liked* the Netherwhere.

"So . . . do you see a lot of dragons out here?" London said, excitement making him bounce a little on the balls of his feet.

Tanner and the captain exchanged a look.

Otter met his eyes and said, "Don't you know no one believes in dragons. There's a crew full of people, actual adults, who will say you hit your head during the storm and imagined it. So if you go telling anyone you saw a dragon, people will laugh." She poked his shoulder. "You see the problem, yeah?"

London grinned. "I don't care what they believe! The *last* strange creature I saw was a tentacled thing that snatched my tongue for a squeeze. Don't expect anyone would believe me about that—or about the chimera I met. But I know what I *know*."

No one spoke for a moment that seemed to stretch out far too long. They stared at him.

"What do you really do out here?" he asked.

"Collect dragon skins," Otter said. "The skins are worth a *lot*. We have direct orders from the queen to do so—and not to admit that dragons exist."

"You *skin* dragons?" London stepped backward, suddenly not sure he wanted to be around these people after all. "That's—"

"*No!*" Otter grimaced. "They shed. They're just big lizards. If we don't gather the skins, people could learn they were out here when the shed bits wash into shipping lanes. And *other people* might hurt the dragons. We don't. Plus"—Otter smiled widely—"I can tell when the dragons are near, so we can sail out here where others can't. I, um, talk to dragons . . ."

London thought about his friend Algernon. He talked to creatures, too. "Makes sense. Someone else I know can communicate with magical creatures."

Suddenly London missed his friend, but Algernon was training to be a Raven, and Ravens don't really get to have friends.

"Do they talk the way gargoyles do?" he asked.

"Gargoyles talk to you?" Otter's eyes got wide, as if that was exciting.

"Not me, just my friend," London admitted. Nothing talked to London. He was perfectly ordinary, unlike both Algernon and Otter. He shoved that thought away and asked, "What do the dragons talk about?"

"Nothing yet. I talk, and I think they *hear* me, but no replies. Kelpies, though . . ." Otter shuddered. "*Never* answer a kelpie. They don't shut up. Dragons are quiet. I *feel* them, and *I* talk to *them*, but they're silent."

London looked through the porthole at the sea. Knowing that there were kelpies and dragons under the water made everything scarier—but it also made it seem even more exciting and beautiful. Just like the Netherwhere.

The captain cleared his throat. "Well, then. Let's get some vittles."

"Wait." Otter shook her head. "London, you said you met a chimera. I know there are kelpies, and gargoyles, and faeries, but a *chimera* . . . ?"

London held up a hand like he was about to make an oath. "I swear there is! The chimera isn't as big as that dragon that almost drowned us, but they're scarier than most things I thought could exist outside nightmares."

"A chimera? In Glass City? I don't think so," scoffed Tanner. He motioned London toward a chair and told Otter, "Sounds like your stowaway is having a heat fever or something."

"Not there. I was in the *Netherwhere*." London plopped down in a chair, an honest-to-goodness chair like in Nightshade Manor. The difference being that *this* chair was bolted to the deck of a ship.

London looked around and saw most things in the captain's quarters were anchored down in one way or another. Even the bookshelf had crossbars over it so the books wouldn't fall. He could see this was necessary because the few things that weren't fastened down had been rattled in the storm and dragon encounter. The bedcovers were on the ground in a heap, and a sword was dangling from a light fixture on the ceiling like it had gotten snagged there when the ship tilted.

The captain reached up and poked the sword. He caught it by the hilt and was still holding it when someone rapped on the door.

"Enter," he bellowed.

Crew members carried in platters of fish, cheese, and bread. London's stomach growled at the sight. He was about to take a bite of his bread when Otter nudged him. She was passing out wet strips of cloth with orders to "clean up."

Captain Maul and Tanner cleaned their hands and looked pointedly at him.

London obeyed, and then, once the crew was gone, London said, "So the kelpies have a lot to say, huh?"

Otter snorted. "They talk until I can't barely sleep some days. Gargoyles in the cities talk a bit, but they're not chatty. *Nothing* talks like a kelpie." She grabbed a chunk of some sort of fruit. "I threatened a herd of them. Said Da would squish them with the boat. Not that he could, yeah? Still, they do go on."

"Hard to talk around a chatterbox." Tanner winked at Otter.

Captain Maul laughed, and Otter poked the captain's arm with her fork. A twinge made London look away. He had no real memory of a father, just him and his mother, and she'd been gone for years. His most recent family was the house of thieves where he'd grown up, and then—for a brief time—at Nightshade Manor, where London had been brought to work for the alchemist. That was where he'd befriended Algernon Nightshade.

"I bet you could talk to other creatures, too, if you met them," London said.

Otter opened her mouth to say something, but the door burst open. In a flash, the captain had his sword raised. London was impressed—Captain Maul would've made an excellent thief with reflexes like that.

A man came sliding into the room, hat in hand. "Captain, we're taking on too much water. The crack in the hull just widened. The patch slid out, and we're"—the ship gave a lurch—"sinking! And some of the lifeboats aren't seaworthy after that tussle with the lizard. There aren't enough . . ."

Captain Maul pointed at Otter. "You get to a lifeboat. Tan, go with the kids and make sure they get a seat."

"The bilge pumps aren't keeping up," yelled a voice from the deck. "Can't pump out the sea itself!"

"Da!" Otter jerked away from Tanner. "I'm not leaving you."

"Ottilie—"

"Wait," London said to Otter. "Why don't we go to the Netherwhere? If you can connect with the dragons, maybe you can ask Ebba to open a door to get us there."

She stared at him, mouth open, as if he'd suggested the most ridiculous thing ever.

"I've *been* there, Otter," London said. "What's the harm in trying?"

CHAPTER 7

◆——————◆——————◆

Sofia

The House of Florence, like all the dwellings in the underground, was often chilly. Their firepit kept it from being painfully cold and made shadows flicker on the walls as thieves jostled or wrestled.

Sofia looked around at the group and at Florie sitting on a sofa like an uncrowned king. This was her family, and they were all happy to be here. They'd all been left to figure out how to survive when their parents had died, were transported, or abandoned them. Sofia had one parent dead, and one parent who'd been shipped off with other prisoners. After her dad was taken away, she had hoped the lady who lived with them might keep her, but she'd tossed Sofia out. For a while Sofia didn't belong anywhere.

Then she discovered a life underground. Being in Florie's house had saved Sofia.

"We need to figure out what's going on with these new ships," Florie announced. A torch nearby made his face look like it was glowing. "Who ordered them? Where are they taking kids? And why *now*?"

Thieves looked up at him, but no one said anything.

"We'll take shifts rescuing kids," Florie continued. "We can meet with the other thief houses to make plans. We'll need more food if we are to swell our numbers, but luckily there's still plenty of room in the underground to expand. We'll work to face this as we have the cold and hunger."

Instead of arguing, the kids were nodding and murmuring as if this were the start of a new adventure. Kids stood. Others raised hands. Everyone was willing to do their part.

Florie motioned to her and Rio. "Sofia has saved this one. But plenty of others were taken to sea, right, Rio?"

"Yes, sir." Rio's voice was loud and angry. "They said they were going to feed us to the kelpies. And I am not wanting to be horse food."

Florie nodded. "*No one here* is meant to be horse food."

Kids cheered.

"What do we do when they try to starve us?" Florie chanted.

"Take!"

"And what do we do when they try to catch us?"

"Hide!"

"And what do we do for our brothers and sisters who haven't yet learned how to take and hide?" Florie yelled.

"Save them!"

"Exactly." Florie smiled at the group of kids.

Sofia knew that the adults aboveground had no idea how strong children could be when they worked together. There were far more kids in the underground than the adults realized. And they had banded together in their thief houses, coexisting in peace, not fighting for territory.

If the adults weren't going to help the kids—and even worse, sent them to die at sea—the kids were here to fix things themselves.

CHAPTER 8

❖ ❖ ❖

Otter

London and Otter stood together on the deck of the H.M.S. *Tempest*. The sea was calm—though the crew was anything *but* calm as they tried to save the *Tempest*.

Every so often the ship would lurch as the water flowed into the hull faster than the pumps could expel it. The crew was running a bucket brigade to help buy the captain time to decide what to do, but that was like thinking a cork would stem a gash in a vast barrel. They were sinking.

"Netherwhere? You want us to go to the *Netherwhere*?" Otter looked at London. "How would we even get there?"

"I don't know *how*, but my friend did it. He goes there all the time," London explained quickly. "And he talks to creatures like you do."

"Uh-huh."

"I've been there! I swear it! It's how I knew about dragons. Not just dragonets, but big swooping coin-collecting—" He stopped, a sick look coming over him.

"What?" she asked.

London shook his head. "I might, sort of, have carried a bag of gold coins onto the ship."

Otter glared at him. "You can't have *gold* at sea. Every fool and his uncle know that. Silver. Bronze. Steel. They're okay. Not gold. Never *ever* gold."

"I didn't plan to—and I thought the gold thing was just a superstition," London said. "I was going to pay for my ticket with my gold. Then no one asked me to pay, and I was on this ship and . . . I'm sorry."

Otter glanced at her dads. They were arguing while gathering the things they hoped to save before the ship sank, a few pictures and their sailing papers.

Otter grabbed London's arm and pulled him to the opposite side of the deck. "Toss it, now!"

London pulled his bag of coins from an inside pocket and separated the gold ones. They gleamed in his hand—his future—the money to pay for the food and shelter he'd have in Northland. But he knew Otter was right. He couldn't risk jeopardizing the crew.

He dropped the coins into the sea, and he and Otter watched them sink under the surface, only to see a gleaming eye as big as a wagon wheel stare up at them. It seemed to wink, and then it and the gold were gone.

"Do you see . . ." London whispered. He waved at the dragon.

"Thank you," Otter said.

Then a yell from Otter's dads, who were arguing in louder and louder voices, drew their attention.

"You're a goat!" Tanner snapped at the captain.

The captain pointed toward the lifeboats. "The crew will go into the boats first. If they all get to the boats, then maybe I—"

"They're *already* prepared to go." Tanner pointed to the assembling crew on deck, who were almost done readying the lifeboats, gathering food and flasks of water. "Well-trained lads and lasses. If we *order* them to go, they will. We can have some of us take shifts floating in the sea, hanging off the rafts, and then switch out. We'll make it work."

"A captain stays with his ship and—"

"Nonsense!" Tanner yelled. "You will not go down with this ship!"

Otter tugged London away from her fathers. "How did he do it? Your friend? How did he get to the Netherwhere?"

"Call out to Ebba. That's the creature in charge, the chimera. I think my friend called out for Ebba, like you do with dragons, maybe . . . He said he called out in his mind, and then there was a door to go through. It appeared."

When Otter gave him a look, London added, "I went through a door with him. It's real. I swear it. I met Ebba, the chimera, and everything."

Otter turned away to stare out over the long stretch of sea. "Where am I to find a door here?"

"Anything that has an opening?" London asked.

White tips rose here and there in the water. Storms or kelpie manes, she wasn't sure what they were. There weren't a lot of options left. Sink with the ship, get in a lifeboat, or . . . try this.

"Da? Tan?" Otter said, trying to sound braver than she felt. Both of her fathers turned to her.

"I'm going to try . . . a thing to stop this."

"All right," the captain said. "But there's not much time . . ."

"Ebba? If you're out there, I could use a gateway," she thought-spoke, closing her eyes and imagining an opening to another world.

She heard London's voice. "Promise we'll deliver cookies as thanks."

"Cookies?"

"Red wet cookies," London said. "Tell them we'll bring cookies like Algernon Nightshade does."

"My friend London says we'll bring cookies like Algernon Nightshade if you help. Otherwise we'll all sink . . . or get eaten by dragons or—"

"Dragons?" A voice startled Otter and asked, "What do *you* know of dragons?"

"They're beautiful, shimmering, and strong . . . but now we're sinking from the claws of one."

The voice felt massive inside her mind, as if all the sounds in the world had sunk into the belly of a drum. It was a heavy voice, deep and old. "And you want a door because of dragons?"

"Yes! A door! I don't want my family to die, or the dragons to get caught because we get sunk," Otter added. "Please, help us."

"Ottilie!" the captain called.

Then members of the crew started to call out or gasp.

"Captain!"

"Look at that!"

"Where'd the Maelstrom come from? It's not supposed to be *here*!"

"Are we off course?"

Otter opened her eyes, and there it was. A doorway. In the center of the Maelstrom, at the end of a twisted tunnel, was an opening. She couldn't see the other side, but she knew it was a doorway.

"We need to go *there*!" Otter pointed at the churning water and felt its pull. "Da, go through it! Take the *Tempie* into the heart of it."

If they ignored her, she thought she might be pulled inside out herself. She felt like a hook had snared her under the ribs. Guiltily, Otter thought it must be what fish felt like when a hook caught them. She might never eat another fish.

"Fish are delicious," the voice said.

Otter decided not to reply. She simply stood, holding the connection to that voice, and waited. Members of the crew were adjusting the battered sails, and others were pulling the emergency oars.

"You sure, Ottilie?" Tanner asked from her side.

She nodded. "Please? Go toward it. I'm *certain*."

"Full speed ahead, Captain!" he called out. "Our daughter says we must!"

And the ship sailed forward until the first sliver of wood touched that glimmered space, the doorway to another world.

No more than the first grain of wood had made contact when suddenly the ship surged forward as if a massive wave had caught the boat and started spinning it.

"Tethers!" multiple voices called out. "Lash in!"

For a brief, sickening moment, Otter was sure they'd be spun into oblivion by the water funnel, but then she opened her eyes to see them tipping to sail down a waterfall.

That was *so* much better.

"Tethers!" voices called again.

The lashings they had for dragon encounters were essential as the entire ship fell through the sky. All around them was air, but in it was the splash of water pouring downward. Fish and tangled seaweed joined them, sliding past.

There shouldn't be waterfalls in the center of the sea, but Otter couldn't deny what had happened. They had fallen through a water funnel in the sea, dropping slower and slower down a waterfall.

When the ship landed with a giant splash, they were barely moving. No shattering hulls or tearing sails. The *Tempest* tilted and wobbled, but she didn't sink. And there, not too far away, was a beach with sand nearly as blue as the sky.

"Land ho!" Tanner shouted, pointing at the beach.

Everyone lined the rail; they were soaked and dripping with seaweed. A few fish flopped across the deck. To a person, the crew looked stunned.

But Otter . . . she felt like every holiday had come at once. She felt like lightning was inside her skin. Her whole body was sparkling and warm. She grinned at the sight of the green-tinted water and strange waterfall that still poured down into the bay. Fish rained into the sea, and the air tasted like sugar instead of brine.

London leaned closer and said, "Welcome to the Nether-where, Otter."

CHAPTER 9

❖———◆———❖

London

London squinted as he stared all around them—the calm bay, the green sea, the blue sand. Things rippled under the water's surface, streaks of color that might as well have been living jewels.

"Dragons," London said, trying to keep his words short because he remembered the difficulty breathing in the first few minutes here. The last time he was here, the air felt more like water at first, but Algernon said the arrival experience and place of entry always varied, and he never knew where he might land.

Otter met his gaze. "Where?"

He pointed at the scaled things under the water, taking a moment to concentrate on breathing.

Otter shrugged. "Maybe some came through with us?"

"It's brilliant, isn't it?" London whispered, grinning at the sheer oddity of it all. Assorted gargoyles swooped in the sky as they did in Glass City, but here clouds of faeries darted around like fanged insects, a group of young kelpies played in the surf, and something that looked like an enormous cat leaped from tree to tree.

"Yes, mostly, except that there's a *giant* slug over there making a loud, *horrible* noise." Otter nodded toward a globby thing gargling on the beach. The slug was as big as a horse, and its head was covered with eyestalks; each stalk was lined with tiny little eyes in all directions.

As the ship heaved closer to the beach, the gargling grew louder and louder.

"I think it's sounding an alarm," London said, louder this time as his lungs filled up with Netherwhere air and started to work right.

"Now what?" Otter said.

"We get to shore. No one drowns." London watched for the chimera. Would Ebba even greet him? Would they decide that their lack of cookies was grounds to eat them?

"Do we have any meat?" London asked Otter. "Is there anything like that on the ship?"

"Meat for . . . ?" Otter asked.

"Ebba. The chimera. That's who opens the door," he whispered. "We need raw meat to thank them."

Otter directed a crew member to find some meat, and they took off to do what she wanted. She'd saved the ship and the crew, so London wasn't surprised at how fast they obeyed.

The ship ran aground with a thunk, and London grabbed the railing.

"Steady!" the captain called out. Then he nodded to Tanner.

"Anchors down, lads," Tanner added.

"Drop the lifeboats, and we'll head to shore!"

London looked away from the creaks of ropes lowering tiny boats to the bright-green sea and realized the slug was oozing off into the dark forest that bordered the beach.

"It's leaving." London pointed. "The slug."

"Is that a good thing or bad?" Otter asked.

Several crew members glanced at him, clearly having the same question.

And London felt rather special, having people look at him like he was the one with the answers. "Either they're just leaving or going to go tell others we're here. Either way, the slug is not attacking us. *That* part's good."

"Fighting slugs sounds gross," Otter said before looking around. Loudly, she called, "Boats, mates. You heard the captain."

Captain Maul stayed on the swaying ship, and Tanner took the first boat to shore. With only three undamaged lifeboats to ferry people, London realized that if the ship had gone down, most of the crew wouldn't have had a seat.

Once they were all on shore with their supplies, the crew began to gather driftwood. Soon, fires were blazing, and Captain Maul was giving instructions.

"London," Tanner called out. "C'mere, lad."

Otter stayed beside him as they went over to her dads.

"So now what?" Captain Maul asked. "Where do we go on this island? What do you know?"

"We must find Ebba," London suggested. Then he repeated it more surely: "Ebba, the chimera. They're in charge. So we need to go see them."

Otter's dads exchanged a look. Then the captain said, "In

the morning, we can investigate this . . . chimera. It's getting late now, and I'm not going into those woods with no light and no idea what's on this island. It wasn't even on my map."

"Da, that's because it's not in our world. We're in the *Netherwhere*," Otter said.

Captain Maul paused, looked at Tanner again, and then shrugged before he said, "Ottilie, it's just an island. They form from the magma under the sea."

"And the slug?"

"Bigger than usual, I'll say, but we often encounter strange things." The captain hugged her close. "We got turned around in a water spout. That's all."

"Sure, Da," Otter said, with a roll of her eyes in London's direction.

London grinned at Otter. At least his new friend realized where they were. He wasn't sure now if Tanner or any of the crew did, but the girl who could talk to dragons believed him. That counted for a lot.

CHAPTER 10

◆———◆———◆

Marian

Her land beast was gone. Vanished. It wasn't Marian's goal to sink *her*, not the Otter. She might sometimes poke holes in the wooden bellies of other ships, but only the ones that endangered the hatchlings or were stealing her fish. Her food. What was she to do? The ones at the edge of what the land creatures called the Crimson Sea scooped them up in their nets and flopped them on the planks of their vessels. They weren't even eating them.

She'd watched.

Of course Marian wouldn't sink the Otter's ship! Sometimes she or the other dragons got a little too close to her, but Marian had sworn to protect *all* little hatchlings, including the Otter. She might have sprouted legs and walked on land, but she was theirs. A dragon in the wrong shape is still a dragon.

Today, though, *shiny* things were calling out to them. No dragon resisted shiny things well.

Marian had tried to keep the younger dragons away. She'd been doing fine, but then she misjudged how close *she* was. Too close. Her claws too sharp. Her tail too fast.

Then the ship had a hole, and the sea went into it.

Maybe it was time for the Otter to join them? The girl wanted to be in the waves, too. Marian heard it, her longing and hopes. Some creatures weren't made for dry land.

Dragons weren't.

The Otter wasn't.

When the Otter was smaller, Marian used to be able to convince her to come off the boat, and they'd swim together.

When the seas were still, Marian had sometimes made waves for the Otter.

When kelpies came too near, Marian used her talons to scare them away.

"Where are you now?" Marian called for the Otter.

She had tried so very hard to not interfere too much or ask questions of the Otter. The Otter was in the shape of the land folk, and Marian had ordered the others to respect that. It was hard when the Otter called to them. Marian wanted so badly to reply, to talk to her.

But today Marian *had* to reply because the Otter's loved ones were in danger. For some reason, the Otter was asking for Ebba's help—as if *that* creature would save her. *Hmph!*

So Marian broke the rules—she spoke to her Otter. *You want a door?* she had offered, and then she had shown the way.

Marian had heaved herself through the door as well. Her

scales scraped this time, and it hurt when the bright green of her blood leaked out.

Many dragons followed. They would be where the Otter was, watch her, guard her.

Now Marian, the great elder of the dragons, felt the familiar pull of the girl . . . who was standing on land.

"Protect my Otter." Marian called out this order to the little nuisances of the air. Dragonets were silly beasts, and most everyone found them infuriating, but they were *still* dragons. They would obey Marian, and they were near enough to the Otter to protect her now.

As for the dragons who'd come with Marian, they splashed in the sea and waited. Their Otter never stayed long on land, and when she was back in the water, they'd be near her once again.

All hatchlings must be kept safe, protected by dragons' wings, but the Otter especially needed guarding, as she had no talons or wings or scales to protect herself right now.

Someday she would, and then the Otter would realize what a magical creature she was.

CHAPTER 11

◆———◆———◆

Sofia

Once Sofia was certain no one was watching her, she slipped away from the thieves who were swapping tales and showing off their daily hauls. Everyone would have to put their stolen goods into Florie's baskets, but a lot of the kids liked to compare their stuff before they turned it in. Today Sofia wanted to turn her loot in as soon as she could.

The youngest kids were starting to line up for their meals. Once they filled their plates, the rest were allowed to approach the kettles and serve themselves. Hot food and hot fires, both kept a person a little warmer.

"You all good, Sofia?" Rott asked as he appeared at her side. He was younger than her, and it had been years since he had brought her to Florie's, but Rotterdam never stopped looking out for her.

"Yes, I just need to go drop off my stuff." Sofia motioned toward Florie, who was surrounded by empty baskets.

"Mention to Florie I want a shift at the dock, being a rescuer, you know?"

Sofia nodded, but Rott had vanished. Anyway, Florie likely knew. He paid careful attention to all of them.

Sofia walked over and grabbed an empty basket. Carefully, she put her day's take in it: two watches, a half dozen sweet oranges, a block of cheese that had been her riskiest snatch, five onions and a few turnips, and her big haul—a dagger with a black stone on the hilt.

"Here." She handed the basket to Florie.

Florie lifted the cheese first. "Treasure."

Sofia nodded and folded her hands together as she watched Florie discover the dagger. His eyes got wide, and he flicked the stone of the end of the hilt. "An *athame*."

Sofia shrugged as if it was nothing special. She'd left the dagger in its sheath and been careful not to touch the hilt with her bare skin. All she said was "Looks like."

"Can you use it, Sofia?" Florie asked, holding the athame up.

Again, Sofia shrugged. "No one ever taught me."

He unsheathed it. The blade looked like it had the same black stone pressed into the center groove. "That sounds like a yes."

When he held the athame out toward her, Sofia had to cross her arms to keep from reaching out. It felt like the short blade was calling her name. Magic, power to make the world change, started rippling under her feet, asking her to let it in.

"Go on." Florie flipped it around so it was hilt toward her. "Show me you can, and it's yours."

An athame was worth a lot of money. He could sell this and earn a lot for the House of Florence.

But Sofia couldn't help herself any longer. She snatched the athame before he changed his mind. It had no more than touched her skin when Florie jerked back. The ley line nearest their pocket of the underground was thick. Magic surged toward her so quickly that her hair floated.

Not all magic was the same, and Sofia hadn't learned how to do much of anything with it. She'd experimented, but without any training or an athame to focus the energy, she was only fumbling around with instincts.

Reacting to the feeling that she was a jug that was overflowing with magic, she shoved it outward thinking, *Warm.*

The whole of the underground felt warmer, as comfortable as if it were a sunny summer day.

Florie stared at her and stretched. "That feels nice. How long will it last?"

Sofia shook her head. "No idea."

"Come with me," he ordered.

Sofia followed Florie as he rolled his chair to the next-door building that was his place. It must have once been the home of a wealthy family. An ornate thin rug covered the floor, and there were shelves with books and a picture. Florie had made part of it into an office and brought in a sofa and a heavy wooden table and chairs.

Now he led her to an area that housed a giant tub with feet. It was filled with water, and its outside was fire-blackened.

"My mother used to use wards to heat the water. Can you"—he motioned to the tub—"do that?"

Sofia tugged on that same ley line, pulling the energy

needed to do magic, but slowly so she was only drawing a sip of it, not a big gulp this time. Too much, and the water would boil.

Sofia pushed the energy where she wanted it by aiming the tip of the athame. In a moment, the water looked cleaner, and she stopped when it started to steam.

She wasn't entirely sure how the magic worked, or if it always would. It used to be that her ability to change the world only happened when she was angry or scared—and afterward she would feel like something thick and furry was stuck in her throat. It had made Sofia very careful not to feel things too much.

The athame changed everything. It gave her a way to aim the energy she pulled from ley lines.

Carefully, she tested the water with the back of her hand. "It's hot, but not *too* hot."

Florie nodded, and she could see by the way he smiled that she'd impressed him.

"The athame is yours," he said. "I am grateful to you, Sofia. The warmth helps my legs. The cold makes them ache."

"Cold bathing isn't pleasant," she agreed.

Florie dropped a paper ball into the steaming water. It looked like the scented ones the nobs bought in the city. Maybe it even was, but Florie was looking at the water the way the youngest of the thieves looked at candied plums.

And then he turned his head to Sofia and stared at her. "It's interesting. Merry Ward, who used to be part of the House of Moscow, is good at wards, too."

"Of course," Sofia said. "That's why she's at Corvus School

for the Artfully Inclined now. Training to be a Raven. Everyone's heard of *her* . . ."

"Yes, but you know, you also *look* just like her."

"I know," Sofia said. She had noticed her resemblance to Merry when the other girl had once visited the House of Florence. Sofia had hid, and nobody else had said anything.

It couldn't mean anything, could it?

Then she got called Merry out on the street a few times, and after that, she wore scarves to hide her hair and face whenever she left the underground.

Were they sisters? Twins, even?

Sofia couldn't let herself dream of a sister. But she couldn't stop thinking about how there was another girl who looked like her—and *that* girl *worked* wards.

And so, it appeared, did Sofia.

CHAPTER 12

Otter

"G uards," Tanner barked. "Two to a team. Patrols, too. Sleep in shifts."

Something in the nearby forest giggled, and the gargoyle in the tree nodded at Otter as if they were old friends.

Otter was sitting still as she typically did on land, but she couldn't help noticing that she felt surprisingly *good*. She was never comfortable on land, so Otter was dumbfounded that she felt perfectly fine here.

Then a dragonet perched on her lap and stared up at her. It gave her what appeared to be a smile and burped in her face.

"Ewww!" Otter waved a hand between them. "Your breath smells like eggs. *Bad eggs.*"

The dragonet turned its back to her and shook its orange bum in her direction, tail wagging. Tiny little sparks filled the air as it departed.

"It burped *and* farted at me!" Otter stood up, and four more small dragonets darted at her. One sat on each shoulder, one darted around her in circles, and one settled atop her head. "Ow!" she said as its talons caught in her hair.

"Otter?" London had finally noticed.

The dragonet that had been circling her spit fire at London's backside, and he ran forward. Then another dragonet sparked her backside, too.

Otter pulled out her ship's knife and pointed it. "Stop, or I'll tell the crew you'd be delicious roasted, yeah?"

Something about the dragonets made her angrier than she could explain. She didn't mind most creatures, but these little menaces were *farting and spitting fire* at them. She was furious.

"I think they might be trying to steer us," London said.

"Well, *real* dragons can communicate with me . . ." Otter said.

At that, all four dragonets lined up behind her and nudged with their beaks. One darted forward and nudged London.

"Well, I guess they do understand you," he muttered. "How about we let them lead us rather than burn or shove us?"

She glanced back at the beach. Everyone was busy.

Otter nodded. If there was a dragon, or dragonet in this case, leading her somewhere, she wasn't going to ignore it. Following proper-sized dragons had always let the ship find the best currents. Maybe following these dragonets would be wise, too.

She looked at the dragonets and said, "Lead on!"

She and London clambered over trees and rocks and hopped across a stream. They'd both eaten and drunk only things they had with them, but Otter was looking at that water thinking it would be good to have fresh water. She crouched down and cupped it into her hands. She held it up and sniffed. The water smelled like nothing, not salty or foul.

She was about to drink it when London offered his water flask. "Don't know that I'd drink *anything* here."

The dragonets were zipping around and motioning at the water. That, more than anything, made her accept London's flask.

Otter glanced back and could barely see the trail. She probably should've told someone where they were going, but her fathers were always convinced there were dozens upon dozens of dangers if she was out of their sight.

The forest opened into a wide flat meadow, complete with a burbling brook and flowers of many sizes and colors. Some of those flowers held faeries, and Otter flinched. A faery infestation was every ship's nightmare. They had rows of sharp, needle-like teeth, and most people spent a whole trip sick if they got a bite from an angry faery. Luckily, she'd never been bitten.

At the center of the clearing, the dragonets popped out of existence, as if they simply vanished. She'd seen creatures submerge in the sea, but never disappear in the empty air.

"Did you see . . . ?" London gestured around them, where not a single dragonet could be seen.

Now the air was loud with a *whirr whirr whirrrr* noise as more faeries arrived and hovered over blossoms before settling down to watch them.

"They're usually the ones in your face," London whispered, watching the faeries. "Why are they being . . . calm?"

Then, all at once, every single buzzing insect-like faery smiled at the same moment. London flinched, bracing for an attack that didn't come.

"You weren't expected," said a rumbling voice. The owner of the voice appeared to be a three-headed *something*. There was a lion head with a fluffy mane, and a goat's head that had something tucked behind one ear, and a snake head that was hissing at the faeries.

"Hello, Ebba," said London. He bowed deeply and pulled at Otter's arm. She refused. She had a tickling in her mind, a strong insistence that *she* did not bow or curtsy. Not to this creature, not to any creature.

"Good Otter," came a soft voice.

"Was that you?" she asked Ebba. "In my head just now."

"A chimera is *not* a dragon," the lion head said, as if that answered anything at all. "And I do not whisper."

"Marian," the goat head bleated. "Maaaarian is home."

The snake shook all over like it was trying to slither off the rest of the chimera. "Go to shore! Musssst see Marian!"

The lion growled and snapped its teeth at the snake and then at the goat. They both stilled, and then the lion turned to stare at Otter.

"Everyone bows to me, but not you. *You* are still a rude beast." The chimera charged forward, scuffing the ground and scattering faeries and blossoms.

"What?" Otter tilted her head, meeting the eyes of each

head. "I just arrived. I'm new to your"—she waved around the area—"world, so how can I be *still* rude?"

The chimera sighed from all three heads at once. "So you aren't truly home?"

"Um . . ." Otter pointed behind her in the general direction of the green sea where the *Tempest* was floating. "I'm *always* home. I live on a ship, so I'm home everywhere we sail. Didn't I just ask you for a gate, and you answered?"

The lion head was towering directly over her now, staring down with teeth gleaming. "Not I. But why are you here in the Netherwhere, anyway?"

Otter felt more irritated than scared. She crossed her arms and glared up at the growling lion head. The snake head peered around the top of the fluffy mane—but the goat sounded like it was *snoring*.

"A dragon poked a hole in my family's ship, and we were sinking. *He*"—Otter pointed at London—"said his friend had opened doors to here, and so we tried. I tried. It worked, so now we're here."

She held her hands wide. To be honest, she had absolutely no idea how she'd truly ended up here, but she figured that was beside the point. She was here. The creature in front of her was in charge, and for some reason, the chimera thought she knew about things she didn't.

"I did not answer you, Otter," the chimera said. Then the chimera looked from her to London. "Who are *you*?"

"London," he said. "I was here before—with Algernon Nightshade."

"Ah. Hello again." The chimera flopped down, startling faeries and stirring dust, and stared at them. "Did Marian send you?"

"Marian?" London echoed. "Who's this M—"

"Dragon." Ebba nodded all three heads at once. "She is a dragon, probably the one that brought you here. I thought Otter was ready to come home, but Marian is probably the problem. She is *often* the problem."

"What do you mean, 'come home'?" Otter stared at the creature.

"Back to the Netherwhere." The chimera reached out one great paw as if to pat her. "With your family."

"You're *from* here?" London stared at Otter.

"I am *not*," she whispered. "The chimera is confused. Faery venom, maybe? Bad diet? Hard to say, but . . ."

All three chimera heads began to laugh, and the mix of sounds was one of the creepiest things she'd ever heard. Goat laughter—which involved bleating noises and snorts—wasn't terrible, but lion laughter was a sort of coughing, scary noise. The snake's laughter was the worst. It sounded like someone had a dried gourd or baby rattle and was shaking it as hard as they could.

"You *are* from here, Otter," the snake head whispered. "Such a silly egg."

"Forgetful," the still-giggling goat said. "Lost little eggling."

London shivered and gave her a strange look, like he was searching for wings or scales or something.

Otter glared at all of them. "I'd know if I was from here."

"Do you remember being an, errr, *egg*?" London asked.

"An . . . *egg*?" Otter blinked at the sheer silliness of the idea. "Girls do not hatch from eggs."

"Some sorts," the snake head insisted. "Scaled sorts. Small sorts. Sea serpent sorts."

"I'm a *girl*," Otter insisted.

"But you *do* talk to dragons," London whispered.

"No! Are you listening to this, London? We are both talking to a chimera right now, for goodness' sake!" Otter gestured at the chimera. "Talking to a creature doesn't make me that. I talk to you, and I'm not suddenly a boy. Clearly, I am *not* a dragon."

"Today," Ebba said with a shrug. "Tomorrow, well, we shall see."

And Otter was not sure what else to say, so she repeated, "I did *not* hatch. I am not a dragon."

The chimera merely smiled at her—which was the worst sort of argument. It was such an *adult* thing to do. Smile and say nothing! How can anyone argue when the other person, or chimera, wouldn't even use words?

And London continued to stare at her as if she might have scales. "Ebba knew your name," London whispered. "Are you positive you're not a dragon? It *would* be super-cool . . ."

Otter couldn't believe this. She might not know everything, but surely being a scaled, water-dwelling, enormous beast was the sort of thing one noticed. It wasn't a detail a person could hide, right?

Some of the crew thought she was secretly a ward worker, because connecting to dragons must be magic. Mostly, though,

Otter thought she was simply a girl who loved the sea and all the things in it—even the kelpies, as long as they didn't start chattering too awful much. Maybe *love* was a kind of magic. It kept the crew safe, and it kept their bellies full, because only they could find the shed dragon skins.

Girls, even magic ones, surely couldn't be dragons. Otter was almost certain of that.

CHAPTER 13

◆——◆——◆

London

London was willing to agree that Otter wasn't a dragon if it meant she would stop arguing with Ebba. "So," he said loudly, hoping to change the subject. "Thanks for whatever part you had in the rescue and, you know, welcoming us to the Netherwhere. We probably should be heading back to the ship now."

Both the chimera and the girl stared at him like *he* was the odd one here.

"Are you leaving?" Ebba's lion head asked.

"Once the ship is fixed." Otter stood taller, clearly not at all afraid of the giant, deadly creature.

"If you are not a dragon, how do you plan to find the door?" the lion head of Ebba asked. "I won't open it, and if you are *not* from here, you cannot."

London frowned. "But Algernon can open—"

"Nightshades are an exception. The Otter is not a Nightshade, and she *says* she is not a dragon, although she did find her way here . . ." The lion head grinned, which looked even scarier than when they were growling.

After a long pause, Ebba added, "When you are ready to speak reasonably, come see me."

Otter stomped away, scattering faeries as she went.

"Do we have safe passage?" London asked, looking hurriedly between the chimera and the girl. He didn't want to lose Otter somewhere in the Netherwhere, but he did want to know if they were safe-ish.

"You? And Otter? Yes." Then Ebba shook their mane. "But we do not welcome adults here. Get rid of them, Friend of Nightshade and Otter."

London almost corrected the chimera, offering up his name again, but he stopped himself. He *was* a friend of Nightshade and Otter, and the way the chimera said it felt like a title rather than a refusal to use London's actual name.

"They can't leave in a leaky ship," London pointed out. Then he wondered what would happen if they didn't get passage out. What would they find if they just set sail here after they repaired the ship? What was out *there*?

Then the lion head exhaled a big *whoosh* of air, scattering the faeries that were still staring at London.

"Go, then, and help get it fixed," Ebba commanded. "And keep the Otter safe."

So London ran through the plants, trying not to stomp blossoms in case of hiding faeries. By the time he caught up with Otter, she had, apparently, stomped her mad away. She was sitting on a moss-covered rock, watching gargoyles swoop overhead.

"You okay?" he asked, flopping against the rock next to her. The moss made it softer than most chairs.

She nodded. "I used to want to be a dragon. I'd dream about it. *Plus*, in my dreams they'd always talk to me. They'd *answer* me. That's just dreams, though, and it was mean of the chimera to tease me."

"So you got mad because you want Ebba to be right?" London asked.

"I guess so, when you put it that way." Otter grinned. "If I was *really* a dragon, I'd never have to go on land. I could swim all day. I could be more help to my dads." She clapped her hands together. "I'd have friends."

London poked her. "I'm your friend!"

"Psh. You are—but only till we get to Northland and you leave." Otter shrugged. "I get lonely with no other kids on ship, yeah? I love my dads, but they're . . . *adults*."

"Could always make friends with the kelpies," London teased. "Shall I call to them?"

"Ugh!" Otter threw an arm over her face. "If you call out to them, I'll . . . I'll . . . lock you back in the cargo where the sea rolls and falls, and you'll get all seasick again—"

"Stop!" London remembered his seasickness too well to even hear her words. "No kelpie summoning. Got it. What if . . . what if I stayed?"

"Here?" Otter sat up straight and looked at him.

"No. What if I stayed on the *Tempest* with you?" he asked.

"Even knowing about dragons and kelpies and storms?"

"Yes."

"What about Northland?" Otter stared at him.

London shrugged. "It doesn't have to be Northland where I live. I just need a new home and job. If I can get both aboard the *Tempest*, why not stay?"

By the time they got back to the beach, London was sure of his decision. Why not life on a ship? Adventure and new places, friends and open seas, the life of a sailor sounded better and better. Sure, there were dangers, but they had powerful friends. Here he was in the Netherwhere chatting with a chimera—and he liked it.

Maybe someday, in some land, he might even find his mother!

But when they reached the shore, London's great mood slipped. Too many children to count were surrounding the camp. They were armed with sticks and spears and slingshots. One girl had what appeared to be a contingent of trained slugs that she was deploying to guard captives.

The crew was at a loss—after all, what kind of adult fights with kids? They looked confused and more than a little over-whelmed as slugs oozed toward them.

"Otter?" London asked.

"Okay, everyone—let's all pause and talk about this!" Otter called out, although London couldn't say who she was talking to, the kids or the crew of the *Tempest*.

London stayed at her side as they marched up to the oldest of the kids, and he asked, "Does Ebba know you're attacking these people?"

"No adults in the Netherwhere!" several kids shouted.

"Get on your boat and go!" yelled a tiny boy, not even tall enough to spear the belly of Captain Maul.

"This is not *your* place!" a girl yelled. "Board your boat and depart, and there will be no injuries."

"Except the ship will sink if they're not allowed to finish fixing it first," Otter said.

The *Tempest* was hoisted on its side with an intricate system of pulleys and ropes so that the men could patch its broken section. Some of the crew dangled over the side of the ship like spiders on lengths of silk.

"Looks like she's patched," London said.

"But she needs to be sealed, too," Otter told him. "We need a mix of brimstone and tar, some swaths of hide, too, if we are going to seal it up right."

"So what do we do?" London whispered, staring at the group of armed children. One girl with long red braids was trying to jab their cook with her spear. "Can you turn into a full-sized dragon and eat them?"

Otter rolled her eyes. "A bit of useful advice, please?"

"Dragons are always meddling," a voice said. "Then Ebba gets angry. *Those* are Ebba's Lost Ones."

London glanced around, realizing quickly that the voice was inside his head.

"Where else would I be? If we speak outside, none of your sort understand." The voice sounded like it was laughing.

"What are you?" London asked, spinning in a circle.

"Really? I answered this already, London," Otter said. "I'm just a *girl*, and this isn't the time. That one there is jabbing Tan, and he's not going to put up with it much longer."

"Not *you*." London pointed at his head. "The voice in here."

"If it jabbers on, it's a kelpie." Otter looked around. "Not sure if faeries even speak."

Then London saw the speaker. He knew without a doubt. A gargoyle was perched in a dead tree, and its stone beak was split in a birdlike smile.

"You?"

"Me."

The gargoyle drifted toward him without a sound. Just like the ones in Glass City, the stone creature moved with as much noise as a feather. Honestly, though, in the Netherwhere gargoyles were one of the least confusing details.

"Tell the Otter to call for Marian," the gargoyle suggested. "The Otter needs Marian."

London repeated the suggestion.

Otter called out, "Marian! Are you here?"

At that, the entire green sea seemed to surge upward. Water sluiced onto the beach, drenching everyone.

And there, crouched like a giant constrictor with shimmery wings and fins, was the largest dragon London could even imagine.

Kids cheered, and the crew of the *Tempest* watched warily.

Then a voice as loud as thunder said, "Welcome home, Otter." The dragon swirled her massive scaled head to look at Otter's dads and said, "Otto, Tanner, how nice of you to visit . . ."

CHAPTER 14

◆——◇——◆

Sofia

Sofia sat in the underground, in what had once been a shop, and thought.

Do I really have a sister?

She'd seen Merry a few times in Glass City as well as when she came underground. Both of them had identical wide blue eyes, thick fringes of dark lashes, and a slightly upturned nose.

While Sofia was staring in the shop's broken mirror, trying to find something on her reflection that was unlike Merry, Florie rolled in.

"I thought you might be here."

Sofia gestured to the mirror. "I do look like Merry. Is that who you see in the mirror?"

"No, I see you, Sofia, not her. She looks like you, but you're not her."

"No, she's guarding the princess," Sofia muttered. "Going to school."

"Do *you* want to go to school?" Florie stopped his chair right behind her.

"I never had a reason to think about it," Sofia said. "I can't even imagine what going to the Corvus School would be like."

"Do you remember anything about your childhood?"

She did, but Sofia had learned not to talk about her life before the streets, because sometimes talking about families made the thieves sad. But now Florie was asking.

"I thought I had a sister once, but my father said she was imaginary," Sofia said. "We were four or five the last time I remember seeing her. She was called Amelia. Then, around that time, I caught the fever. My mother did, too. Mother died, and after a while, I got better. Amelia was mostly at school, and then when Father found a girlfriend, Amelia vanished."

Florie held out a handkerchief, and Sofia realized she was crying.

"Father's friend said I talked to the mirror, not a real girl. But if it was a mirror, why do I remember that we had different dresses on? And why did I miss her so much when she was gone?" Sofia stared at Florie, not quite asking for a hug but wishing he'd offer one.

Sofia knew that thieves didn't hug—but Florie had been there for her since she'd been dropped off in the square with a satchel of food and a spare dress. He held out a hand and patted her hair.

"Anyhow," she said, as if it was fine—even though it wasn't. "It was awful that I never saw Amelia again."

"It was. But I have a feeling you will see your sister again soon. It's good she found a way out and grabbed it. *Lots* of thieves find their own way out. Some through Corvus. Some through being taken to live at Nightshade Manor." He shook his head. "Some, like me, start houses . . ."

"What if I want to stay here and maybe have a house or—"

"Sofia? Maybe you can. Mine will certainly grow large enough to splinter into two groups. We can talk more later . . ." He handed her a bag. "There's something I want to try now. Go over to the cistern and clean up. And put on these clothes. I have a plan."

Then he spun around and left.

When Sofia made her way back to see Florie, she was wearing a dress newer than any she'd ever worn. It was the sort of fancy that made her scoop the bottom up so it didn't collect dirt or tear on the small rocks that were everywhere underground. She had on her own leather boots. They were easy to run in and kept her legs warm all the way up to her knees.

More than a dress had been in the bag, though. Florie had given her a cloak. It was bright green and warm. With it and the athame, she felt ready for . . . something, although she wasn't sure what. Sofia was anxious, but sometimes when she felt that way, it made her able to be brave. Anxious, for her, was just a way to know that what came next was going to be exciting in some way.

Most of the thieves were off to work, but the littles saw her as she walked through the pitted cobblestone streets toward Florie's place.

"You look like a fancy lady!"

"Where are you going, Sof?"

"Do we get dresses too?"

"I feel silly dressed like this," Sofia complained when she saw Florie. "Thieves are to blend in, and *this* isn't blending. I stand out. It's beautiful, but . . . I don't think I can steal things in this."

"Merry *was* a jewel thief, but she's welcome at court now," Florie said. "That means pretty frocks. You will need to be as much like her *as she is now* if you are going to pull this off."

"Pull *what* off? What's the plan? Am I pretending to be her?"

"Yes." He looked at her like he was daring her to argue. "You can get an audience with the queen because of looking like Merry."

"And do what?" Sofia couldn't imagine that breaking into the palace—because that's what it was, even if it was by trickery—would please the queen.

"Just *be* Merry. Tell the queen that we're alarmed by what's happening to the children of Glass City with these new relocation ships. Tell her that we know she wants us to be patient, but things aren't changing fast enough, so you're going to present her with a list of our *demands*."

"You really think I can impersonate Merry?" Sofia stared at him. "But she's . . . poised and knows wards and—"

"I don't believe they'd test you at the door." Florie folded his arms. "You look like her, and you're fast. Pick a pocket. Pull your shoulders back. Meet the queen's gaze."

"Step two . . . ?"

"If she won't listen, steal the queen's jewels. We can sell those for a lot of money. She's a mark, just like any of them that tossed us away. She's worse because she *could* fix it. Some people say the queen's a monster, but Merry insists that she's not, says she's trying to fix things. Merry's plan seems to also be 'wait till she herself is older and has more influence.' But it's all too slow! And kids being sent to sea isn't *fixing* anything."

Sofia swallowed hard. Thieves slid by in the shadows; they didn't confront *queens*. And hadn't Merry already talked to the queen and nothing was fixed? Why would the *queen* listen to Sofia?

"We want no more ships to steal us, and we want them to open regular schools. Those are our terms." Florie kept talking. "Maybe even tell her you heard that the thieves are organizing a rebellion. Offer to negotiate a treaty."

"But—"

"You can reach her! Believe in yourself, Sofia. No one is coming to rescue us, so we have to save ourselves. I believe in you!"

His words made Sofia pull her shoulders back and her chin up. She *could* look like Merry Ward, and she *could* talk to the queen. She would get past the guards, present her terms to the queen, and get at least some of their demands answered.

Or she might get thrown on a relocation ship . . .

Sofia nodded. It was risky, but she had to try. She was uniquely positioned to get an audience with the Glass Queen. "We *do* deserve better, and I'm going to go ask for it."

CHAPTER 15

◆——————◆——————◆

Otter

*T*hat"—Otter knew her hand was shaking as she pointed at Marian—"is a *dragon*, Da. A talking dragon. Do you see her? Scales. Wings. Teeth."

As Otter spoke, the dragon twisted to show off her scales, flapped her wings, and opened her mouth wide so everyone on the beach could see her person-sized teeth. Then she held up a foot and said, "And claws!"

Otter plopped down on the sand and echoed, "And claws . . ."

Her dads were on either side of her.

"My hatchling!" the dragon said.

"Dad? Da?" Otter looked at her parents.

"We should have told you that you were adopted," the captain started.

"She *knows* she's adopted," Tanner snapped. "And she was going to figure this part out sooner or later. I told you she was going to change soon, but you weren't ready. Another trip, you said. Another season, you argued."

"You *knew*?" Otter looked from her da to her dad.

"The sea gave you to us," the captain started. "That part was true."

"You were hurt," Tanner added.

"And there was this giant creature . . ." Captain Maul gestured to Marian. "She asked us to look after you. Said you needed time to heal."

"Your wing tore," Marian's thunderous voice added.

"She, errr, made you girl shaped," Tanner said. "Little like the age you were, but then you stopped remembering being a dragon and—"

"We weren't ready to let go," the captain finished. "We would've told you what you are soon. We just . . . We love you."

Otter started laughing. They had to be joking. She laughed so hard that she started hiccupping.

"Come here." Marian beckoned.

Otter shook her head and scooted away from the water. Whatever was going on, she was not going to go into the sea with the largest dragon she'd ever seen. Her fathers, the dragon, the chimera, maybe they were all playing a giant prank on her.

Or maybe I am a dragon.

Otter shook her head again. Whatever was happening, it would have to wait. She pointed at the beach. "Who are they?"

"Hatchlings. Human ones." Marian settled down in the water so her neck stretched out to the kids, and in a few moments, the lot of them were treating her like their own giant climbing toy. Kids climbed on her and patted her scales.

"Okay . . . they're kids who are in the Netherwhere because . . . ?" Otter folded her arms and stared into one massive dragon eye.

"Maul and Tanner watch my hatchling. I watch these human hatchlings." The dragon shrugged, which was, in fact, the weirdest thing Otter had ever seen. Dragons ought not shrug.

"How did they get here?" Otter knew that not just anyone could open a door to the Netherwhere.

"Got no parents," one boy pronounced. "Snatched and sent to sea."

"Snatchers caught all of us," another explained.

And then several of the Lost Ones started talking all at once. Otter picked up "jump to me" and "a real dragon saved me" and "better than being in a workhouse . . ."

"You rescued them?" Otter asked Marian, wading into the sea.

"Not just *me*. There are too many, so the others did, too. No hatchling should be abandoned," Marian explained.

And Otter thought she might understand a bit more. *All* the dragons in her world rescued kids—and the kids they saved were brought here to the Netherwhere.

"We dragons can't rescue all of them," Marian said, sounding sad. She gestured at the beach with one vast wing. "The bad men don't treat the hatchlings well, so we sink their wooden houses if they are close enough. Just some."

"Sink *some*?" she echoed.

Marian held up an enormous clawed foot and swiped at the air. "Jab. Then take the hatchlings to live here."

"And the sailors . . . ?"

Marian shrugged again. "Ebba says no adults."

"The adults who sink are ones who *steal* kids in Glass City," London reminded her. "They would've stolen me."

Otter thought about the idea of dragons saving kids, of transporting them here, and she glanced at her fathers. "I will have questions, but . . . not now."

Her dads nodded.

Then Otter looked at Marian and added, "For you, too."

"Wise little hatchling," the dragon said.

"Not a hatchling," Otter muttered.

Then she looked around at the kids and the crew of the *Tempest*. "No more spears. No more grumbling. Let's eat and get the ship ready. Then we ask the chimera how to get out of here, and we go."

When several kids frowned, Otter added, "For those who *want* to leave, you can come with us. Maybe some of you have family or a thief house you miss . . ." She glanced at London, who nodded that she was using the right term. Then she continued, "There are jobs on other ships, too, and we can help you find them. But of course, if you want to stay here with the, errr, chimera, that's up to you."

Most of the children cheered, but a few looked at the *Tempest* with interest.

Once the kids no longer shook weapons or jabbed the adults with spears, Otter walked toward the pile of provisions and asked Cook, "What can we make to feed so many?"

Marian helped take care of that by flinging fish to the

cook. And the Lost Ones carried fruits and mushrooms and nut pods from the forest.

When it was mealtime, London plopped down beside her with a bowl of stew. "I wonder if any of the kids will come with us?"

"*That's* what you're wondering?" She gaped at him. "Not, 'Hey, Otter, how's it feel to have scales' or something?"

"Don't see any scales." He shrugged. "I might ask you to swim once you're all dragon shaped or something . . . unless you can fly. Do you suppose you might?"

Otter stared at him. "It doesn't bother you?"

"That you're magical and have two great fathers and a dragon mom?" London paused, chewing the fruit. "I suppose I might be jealous a little. But then again, my friend Algernon has a dad and a brother, but he also has to become an alchemist and brew potions to kill people someday. Prolly a downside to being a dragon, too. Maybe your scales itch? Or you only eat raw fish? Everyone has good and bad in their life."

"Careful, you're starting to sound wise," Otter said. "I hadn't thought about all that. Also, would I be able to switch back? And how strange would it feel to be dragon shaped?" Otter paused for a moment to take a breath. "You know I love my dads, but they kept a secret, and all these dragons refused to talk to me, and—"

"Those are things that happened, not what's next." London shook his head. "I bet every one of the kids here, and the adults, too, have things that happened that were bad. What about what's in *front*, not behind, now?"

Otter looked around. The crew watched Otter and the Netherwhere kids, but Marian the dragon stared only at her. The dragon dozed, but with one eye open. She snored softly, but one giant iris was trained on Otter. It was like both of her fathers' overprotectiveness but in massive size and with claws.

"Would you decide to stay here?" Otter asked London.

"If I was a dragon or"—he gestured with his spoon—"one of them? Or myself?"

"Yes . . . ?"

London snorted in laughter. "I'm still planning to ask for a job on the *Tempest*. But maybe I can also convince a dragon to take me swimming every now and then . . ."

"Hey!" Otter poked him in the side. "I'm not even sure I'm a dragon!"

"Well, your hair is sorta dragon-colored . . ."

"Wait till I have sharp teeth," Otter said as she shoved him over into the sand.

Marian's voice boomed out: "Shall I eat him for you?"

"No!" Otter and London both said, staring up at the looming dragon head. Both eyes were open, and her maw was stretched wide like a serpent about to eat a rodent.

"Fine." The dragon closed her opposite eye this time. "Don't vex my Otter."

They exchanged a look, and Otter whispered, "Vexing is not wise, I guess."

"Luckily, the vexing one here is you," London said in a faux-posh voice.

Then both kids looked at each other and started laughing. Otter was slowly accepting the idea that she might be a dragon. But she was still *herself*—a girl with a friend, dads, a crew, and a ship that needed patching.

After they all finished their meal, Otter was stunned to see assorted planks, bright-green sails, and an iridescent set of nets start to appear. The Netherwhere kids brought out supplies, gargoyles dropped others, and—most shockingly—a flock of dragonets dropped the net on the beach. Admittedly, they dropped it on top of Otter and every dragonet farted loudly and left. Still, it was a sturdy net.

"We will understand if you want to live with your mother for a while," Tanner said as he sat down beside her.

"But we'd *prefer* you live with us," Da added. "Maybe go for dives with her . . . ?"

Otter nodded. She wasn't ready for this, for any of it. Not being a dragon. Not her dads knowing. And definitely not having giant claws and scales.

She stared at her dads and said, "You could've told me, yeah? What if I just woke up a dragon? I'd sink the *Tempest*."

"Fair . . . but you didn't. You're still human shaped." The captain tugged his beard braids. "We would've told you eventually. Just . . . you're still so little."

"She said we'd know when to tell you," Tanner muttered, shooting a glare up at Marian. "And it's not an easy thing to figure out. You have no scales so far! Iffen you even asked about your mum . . . but you didn't."

Otter sighed. Sometimes grown-ups were so silly. "I love

you, and I like staying on the *Tempest*. Maybe one day I'll go stay with her for a while, swim or whatever you do when you're a dragon, but not *now*, though."

She paused. Where did dragons live? What would that be like? Could she switch back and forth between human shape and dragon shape?

"We live a very, very long time, Otter. Much longer than humans. There is no rush," Marian thought-spoke.

And this time, Otter knew that the voice she heard was Marian's. Hers was the voice in Otter's dreams. And when they came to the Netherwhere.

And when she met Ebba.

"Can I even become all dragon shaped?" she asked.

"If you want, Otter. Shall I tell you how?"

And to that, Otter had no good answer. It was exciting, but she couldn't imagine it. Did she want to be a massive, scaled creature?

Or could she be dragonet sized?

"No, Otter, you would not be one of the little monsters," Marian thought-spoke, sounding a bit like she was laughing.

At least she wouldn't be a flying, farting fiend! She looked out at Marian, who was rather majestic. Imagining being like her was still too much for Otter to handle.

She snuggled up between her fathers, looked up at Marian, and told all three of them, "I'm irritated that you hid this, but I still love all three of you."

CHAPTER 16

◆——◆——◆

London

London watched Otter looking at the dragon and knew they were talking. Both Nightshade boys looked like that when the gargoyles or other beings talked to them. London had been a little jealous then, but today he'd spoken to a gargoyle.

Then Otter came up to him and said, "I had to ask about the farting."

"*What?*"

"If it was a dragon thing, I wanted to know," she explained. "Thankfully, it's not. *Marian* says the little dragonets just don't like me on account of my being oddly shaped."

When London stared at her, she added, "*Human* shaped. Wingless."

"Phew," London said. "That's a relief."

And it struck London that here he *was*, actually talking to a dragon. Otter was a dragon. That was pretty special, wasn't it? And he'd met dragons, and a chimera, and slug creatures, and been farted on by dragonets. And almost had a shipwreck before falling through a hole in the sea to the Netherwhere.

He might be ordinary, but *his* ordinary was pretty extraordinary.

He grinned at Otter, not sure what he could say but suddenly happy enough that he hugged her.

When he let go, Otter frowned and patted his shoulder, hard. "There. There. It'll be okay," she said loudly. Then she met his eyes. "Did that help? It's what Tan always says."

Before he could answer, he heard a familiar voice yell, "Look out below!"

London looked up just as Algernon and his old thieving partner, a boy named Milan, popped onto the beach, falling from the sky as if they were feather-light. Behind them, also falling from the sky, were two girls.

"*Milan? Nightshade?*" he yelled as he took a step toward them.

Both girls lifted swords—had they captured Milan and Nightshade?

But then the girls pointed their weapons at London.

Slowly, London held his hands up and stepped back to Otter's side, only to discover that she'd pulled out a long skinny sword and aimed the point of it at *them*. It didn't look like it'd be much use against their swords, but he was hoping there would be no need for swords of any sort.

"He's my friend!" London exclaimed, pushing on Otter's wrist to try to lower her sword. "The one who brought me to the Netherwhere before. That's Algernon! And Milan! Milan was a thief in my house."

All around him, he heard the shivery sound of swords

sliding out of scabbards. He glanced back to see both the crew of the *Tempest* and the Netherwhere kids raising weapons.

The slightly older girl, with the wide blue eyes, asked, "And who are *you*?" She didn't look away as she added, "I thought you said no one came here, guys? This is a lot of kids."

"That's London," Milan said quickly to the girls. "From Florie's house. Safe. *Ours*. Not a threat, Merry!"

Quickly, London drew a thieves' coin out of his pocket and held it up for proof.

The older girl lowered her sword. "Merry Ward, formerly Merry Moscow, thief of the crown jewels."

"Merry *Moscow*?" London echoed. "I mean, Merry Ward."

She was the legendary girl who'd stolen one of the crown jewels. She'd broken into a tower, the second-tallest building in Glass City. And here she was with the son of the Queen's Alchemist and a thief London knew from Glass City.

While he was staring at them in shock, the other girl turned her back and called out, "Ebba? Are you near?"

As London watched, the three-headed chimera galloped out of the forest, moving very much like an enormous lion. The chimera stopped right before the girl with a skid in the sand that stirred up a cloud.

The chimera stretched out, low to the ground. All three heads simultaneously said, "Heir."

The heir? To what?

The girl walked over to the chimera. Even on their belly, the creature was enormous. The girl stepped up and kissed the goat on the forehead. Then she curtsied to the snake—which seemed to be laughing in response. Finally, she walked up and wrapped her arms around the lion head. Her face was hidden in the lion's mane.

"Missed you," she said.

"You were gone for a very long time," the lion head said.

"Daysss and hoursss away from usss!" the snake said, head drooping.

"My sisters send hellos to you," she said before kissing the massive lion head on the nose.

Then she turned to London and Otter. "Who are you? Why are you in the Netherworld? Why is there a boat? Who are these children? And . . . *adults*? Who let the adults in?"

"Ship," London corrected absently, earning a laugh from Otter. "The *Tempest* is a *ship*, not a boat."

"No adults." The chimera glared with all their eyes. "They should be gone soon. Or shall I eat them, Heir?"

"I'm Victoria Wardrop, daughter of Kathleen and Wilbur Wardrop, both Ravens, and cousin to Queen Evangeline," the girl who had hugged the chimera said quickly.

"Vicky's the *princess*," Milan said, gesturing at Victoria with his thumb.

Otter crossed her arms. "I'm Otter Maul from the H.M.S. *Tempest*. This is London. Our ship got a bit of a hole, and we came here so as not to sink." She looked at the boys. "So, there's Merry, Vicky, Milan, and . . . you're Algae?"

Algernon ignored her question. "*You* can open doors to here?"

"Marian is at fault! Let *adults* come here." The lion part of

Ebba roared, and suddenly the sky was filled with a whirring blur of faeries.

Now that he wasn't quite as worried that he'd step on the little beasts and they might poison him with their sharp teeth, London thought they were strangely beautiful.

"Perhaps we should head back," Merry suggested. "I agreed to come, but . . . dragons? An angry chimera? And all these people? I vowed to keep Vicky safe. And you, too, Nightshade. We should go."

Before her friends could answer, Ebba's lion head growled. "I smell a cake."

"A what?" Otter asked in a loud whisper.

"From Nightshade senior," Merry said. "Sorry, I almost forgot."

She pulled a giant tower of raw meat from a bag and held it out toward the chimera. "Master Nightshade says he misses you."

Ebba snorted. "Adult humans aren't welcome in the Netherwhere."

London and Otter exchanged a nervous look.

"*Children* are a gift," Ebba roared. "Adults are not."

Ebba stretched their lion's jaws wide.

"Ca-a-ake," the goat's voice bleated sleepily.

Merry carefully put the entire thing on the lion's tongue. Her hands barely shook, even when Ebba's great maw slammed shut with a squelching noise.

"Please don't be grumpy," Merry said. "We'll sort out these adults and the kids—"

"The children will be fine now. But they were tossed away. Tell your queen about all these Lost Ones!" Ebba's lion head demanded. "Does she know what is going on under her watch? She said she'd do better!"

"My mother rescued them," Otter said, awkwardly gesturing toward the sea, where Marian watched.

"Your mother is a . . ."

"Dragon," Otter said.

No one knew quite what to say to that, but Algernon looked at London with a question in his expression.

London gave a nod. "Truth."

Then the chimera leaped in front of them in a single large bound and raced toward the water, where the *Tempest* and Marian both waited.

As the chimera charged the beach, the children—with their spears and staffs and slugs—let out a loud *whoop!* London watched as they ran like a disordered but energetic army into the sea. A few now straddled slugs, who moved as quickly as serpents but left a shiny trail behind them. The slug slime glowed silver in the evening light.

Several of the child-sized slugs flung themselves into the sea.

And as Otter and London watched in shock, the chimera and dragon had a private conversation that included growls, snorts, spitting, and finally mutual bowing.

"I will aid in the ship repairs," Marian said loudly.

"And I will not eat your adults," Ebba said.

Then Marian gently lifted a slug in her giant claws and tossed it onto the ship. As the slug landed, it started singing. It sang and slid over the boards of the *Tempest*. From the railing on the main deck of the ship, the slug oozed down the side.

As soon as the slug plopped back into the water, Marian fished it out and carefully placed it in the shallow water, where the lost children swarmed it.

Slug after slug slid over the planks of the *Tempest* until the whole ship glistened. London and Otter watched with mouths hanging open.

"Sealed with slug slime," Captain Maul muttered as he came to stand beside them. "Brilliant solution!"

The crew worked through the night, under the watchful, sometimes-snoozing gaze of Marian. It was nearly dawn when her exhausted fathers pronounced the *Tempest* seaworthy.

"And it's sparkling!" Marian added with an unnerving dragon grin.

The ship was, indeed, a glittering thing, blinding in the dawn light. The sails were now wrought of dragon hide woven and stitched together. The colors of the sails were like the ones inside seashells, like opals had been made into cloth.

"She's beautiful! Look at that! Like a gem," Otter whispered.

"You sound exactly like a dragon should, Otter. Drawn to sparkling things . . ." London teased, earning a jab in the ribs from Otter and a stern look from Marian.

CHAPTER 17

◆━━━◆━━━◆

Sofia

As Sofia approached the Glass Castle, she tried to summon all her confidence. Every thief knew how to do two things: be unnoticed and be bold. The first was easier because most adults didn't pay attention to kids. The second was harder.

She must walk as if she had the right to be there. Chin up. Shoulders back. Even steps. The best thieves got by more often than not by behaving as if they *belonged*. They belonged in the shops, and they belonged in the grocers' aisles. That was how they avoided notice. How a person moved was a costume.

"One foot after the other," Sofia whispered to herself as she walked closer to the glowing building. Spires stretched into the sky as if they would pierce the clouds.

As she crossed the stones that led to the waiting guards, Sofia tilted her chin in a way that she hoped seemed haughty. Tonight, Sofia was Meredith Ward, and she must be fearless.

"I need to speak to the queen," Sofia said, voice as firm as she could make it.

"In a rush tonight, missy?" The younger guard smiled as he looked beyond her. "None of the other young devils with you?"

"Not tonight." Her voice quavered a little as the younger of the two guards escorted her into the castle.

"Merry!" another guard called out as she stepped inside.

She nodded. These people knew Merry and spoke to her kindly. This was good. Every thief knew allies were essential.

"Everyone, watch your pockets!" the young guard said, smiling. "Lady Light-Fingers is here."

The guards looked around at them, and one asked, "Who's missing what?"

Sofia quickly stole the nearest guard's athame and held it up. "Someone dropped their dagger."

The young guard laughed. "Dagger, huh? Nice try, Merry. Give Charles his athame."

She smiled as if it were all an act, even though her hands were clenched in fear. Guards put people on deportation ships or in dungeons. If that happened to her, she wasn't going to get away. This was it, the end of her freedom.

The guard led her through an immense room with a floor made of something that looked like shattered glass. She wanted to inspect it, but *Merry* would be used to seeing it, so Sofia couldn't be caught gawking at the floor.

She was led down a long blue-and-gold hallway. Tiny windows high up let in just a bit of light that kept the path bright but prevented anyone from seeing who passed through.

The hallway led to a small door, where another guard waited. The uniform and single black feather in the woman's thick locks identified her as one of the queen's personal Ravens. She tapped a holster of sorts, sewn onto her trousers, and energy surged. A ward worker!

"Ward down," she said.

The guard escorting Sofia motioned to the door.

In mere moments, Sofia was in a room with the queen herself. No servants but one. That one, however, was yet another Raven. She was an older Raven, with black skin, black eyes, black uniform, and that single long black feather in her almost white hair.

"Meredith," the queen said.

Sofia curtsied carefully, or rather tried to do so. Compared to the graceful dip that she'd seen others do when faced with the queen's attention, Sofia was sure she looked like a goose in a dress trying to dance. It was hopeless. Thieves didn't curtsy.

"Tea?" Queen Evangeline gestured, and a table with tea, tiny sandwiches, and pastries was rolled in by a servant, who quickly departed. "Sit, child."

The Glass Queen lifted the teapot and poured for them both. The oddity of the queen pouring tea for Sofia made her want to giggle. Never in her life had she dreamed she'd have tea with the queen—much less see the queen herself serve it.

When she accepted the cup, Sofia slid a ring off the queen's finger in a deft move. It was an impulsive move—a reflex—and she instantly worried that she'd made a huge mistake.

"Pastry?" the queen said, apparently not noticing that she was now missing a ring.

Sofia couldn't help staring at the triple-layered tower of

treats. She'd seen such things in restaurants, but those were for nobs who could sit and sip tea—not thieves who slept in ruins underground.

But these little cakes were for her! Sofia could taste them. All she needed to do was pretend to be someone else and make nice with the queen.

"Help yourself," the queen said.

So Sofia did as she was told. As she bit into a pastry, an explosion of sugar and cream and strawberry filled her mouth. It was the single most delicious thing she'd ever tasted.

"So, this is your true appearance," the queen said.

"Pardon me?"

"If this is your true face, why do you look like Meredith Ward?"

Sofia just about dropped the beautiful little cup filled with hot tea. "I *am* Meredith."

"You absolutely are *not*." The queen peered at her and sipped her tea with the delicacy of someone used to being watched. Elegant. Careful. Then she smiled, but the kindness she'd had in her eyes fled. "So, I ask you again, child, why do you look like Meredith Ward?"

"I actually don't know," Sofia said, shoulders slumping. "I think maybe she's my twin sister. Are you going to call a guard?"

"I knew you weren't her the moment you stepped into the room," the Glass Queen said. "That child would've been trying not to crow over the ring you stole."

Sofia startled. "The . . ."

"Come, now. I know you have a silver ring I was wearing."

The queen ate a little cake with a daintiness that Sofia would never possess. Then the queen said, "Wards, child. I have wards. I always know when your sister steals things. Poisons, illusions, thefts. I'm the queen, so there are always threats. I'm heavily warded."

She leaned back in her chair.

"You, however, are a ward worker. Untrained, from the looks of it. The athame is there, but not bonded to you. So why are you here? Not for theft of a ring."

She stared at Sofia, studying her, before announcing, "No weapons on you, so you're not here to try to assassinate me."

"Assassinate . . . ? *No*. I came to talk with you."

"Did the Collective send you?" Queen Evangeline asked, and there was magic behind that question, pulling an answer out of Sofia.

"No. I just . . . need your help. You're the queen, and that means you're the one who rules *all* of us, not just the nobs."

The Glass Queen made a "continue" gesture.

"We need schools. Proper orphanages. Job training." Sofia's hands shook as she spoke, so she folded them together. "Give us *real* help instead of sending kids away on your ships."

"Ships? What do you mean? I haven't ordered children to be carried away." The queen frowned. "Where did you hear that?"

"I've seen it. I watched a bunch of kids get snatched up and put on the same kind of relocation ships that are used for criminals."

"I did *not* order that! I shall look into it and put a stop to it."

She looked angry, but Sofia didn't think the anger was aimed at her.

"So it wasn't you?"

"No. I would never. But obviously things have gotten out of my control in a number of areas." The queen looked as tired as Florie sometimes did.

Then the queen examined Sofia's face. "You have to be her twin. There's no other explanation for the look—or those light fingers. Now, tell me, do you want to attend Corvus like Meredith? Learn how to handle that athame properly?"

"No. Yes. Maybe?" Sofia accidentally tugged energy from the ley lines under the Glass Castle. The thought of learning excited her, but she wanted to learn to do other things, not just guard the queen. "I mean, I might, but what about my friends? Shouldn't *all* of us have some sort of schooling?"

The Glass Queen tapped her chin with one finger. "How many?"

"Thirty? Forty?"

"Which house?" the queen asked.

"House of Florence, Your . . . ma'am, queen, ma'am."

"So, you want me to enroll *all* of them?"

"Maybe?" Sofia wasn't entirely sure that they'd all want to go. And what about Rott? Picturing the quick-moving boy in a school seemed impossible. Or Florie himself?

"The Corvus School for the Artfully Inclined isn't designed for everyone," the queen said carefully. "It's an elite training program, my personal program for court staff."

Sofia fought the urge to roll her eyes. "Yes, we thieves know all about Corvus. But there are other kinds of schools, too, or there used to be. And I'm not sure what everyone wants. Mostly to not be tossed out on the street. Or have their parents sent off to prison . . ."

"So the empire should have no punishment for theft?"

"We don't commit crimes because we want to. It's because we have to! We need to survive. And we get hungry." Sofia realized her voice was getting loud and tried to calm herself. "Kids have rights, too."

"You sound remarkably like your sister." The queen stared at her. "Although you're far too polite to convince anyone that you *are* her for very long."

Sofia blinked at her. The queen thought she was *polite*?

The Glass Queen stood up. "So . . . thief of the House of Florence, twin to my heir's guard, what is your actual name?"

"Sofia," she said, trying another curtsy, a bit more gracefully this time, she thought.

The queen nodded once. She stepped close enough that Sofia could smell the sweet scent of the lotion or powder that she wore. "Sofia. Maybe it's because I am fond of your sister, or maybe because I've been thinking for a while now about the things you said. I didn't *intend* the schools to close. That was my former advisors. I wanted to not increase the taxes, so they cut programs. Turns out one of them was schools. No teachers complained, and—"

"Maybe because they were all sent away on relocation ships," Sofia muttered. Honestly, any thief could explain these things. Why were adults so unaware of what was happening?

"Yes, well . . . I have been working to undo *many* of their actions, but I can see that it hasn't been fast enough. Being hungry is a horrible thing."

"It is. It would be better if we didn't get so hungry that we had to steal," Sofia said carefully.

"I have baskets delivered to the areas Merry said were passageways . . ." The queen looked at Sofia questioningly.

"Yes, but it's not enough. There are a *lot* of us. It's a start . . . but it's only *one* thing. Where we live, the water for washing is cold. If someone gets sick, we have no tinctures or medicine. We have no proper beds. We need a lot more than bread and parsnips."

"I see." Queen Evangeline nodded. "There is much to do."

Then the queen raised her voice and called out, "Guards!"

Even though the room was sealed and seemed private, with one word from the Glass Queen, several Ravens appeared, including the white-haired Raven and another with eyes so bright they looked like jewels.

"I want guards patrolling the docks. Trusted Ravens. Children are being snatched and sent to sea. If anyone tries that, bring them—and the children—to me."

The guards nodded. Several left, presumably to do the queen's bidding. One guard waited.

After a flash of a smile at Sofia, the queen added, "This is Meredith Ward's sister, Sofia. She will be advising me on a project."

The queen looked back at Sofia and asked, "Is there anyone else you would like to invite to join you?"

"Florie." Sofia knew that her protector would have good ideas. "Head of the House of Florence."

"All right. We will send an escort, and I will convene a committee. Send for Tik and Nightshade," the queen directed.

Then she nodded at Sofia. "You can wait here where there's a nice warm room in which you can relax."

Sofia returned the nod, and then a Raven escorted her through the castle. Was she a guest?

Wrongly or not, Sofia wanted to trust the queen, but the queen had ignored so many of her people for so long. Sofia thought—like most thieves—that trust was a thing you earned.

Still, the queen seemed sincere.

And even though Sofia's plan to trick the queen had failed, it still might lead to the results they needed.

The Glass Queen had *listened*, and that was always a start.

CHAPTER 18

◆——◆——◆

Otter

By the time Marian had sealed all the planks of the *Tempest*—with slime from giant *slugs!*—Otter was sure that things couldn't get any stranger. The ship was sparkling like a gemstone in the green waters of the bay, and children younger and older than Otter were swimming under the watchful eye of the dragon who was, apparently, her mother.

Otter thought about it, about how strange it must have been for her fathers to have a baby dragon plopped down on deck.

"Was I scaly?" she asked, feeling silly but wanting to know.

"Beautifully so—with all the colors of the sea in every scale," Tanner said.

"Why did you keep me?"

"Well, what else would we do? Toss you back? You were hurt," Tanner explained.

Her other dad came over. "Ottilie."

She looked up at the captain.

"Figure out if any of these urchins want to come aboard." He nodded toward the Lost Ones. "Your mother is going to swim us up the waterfall, back to the Crimson Sea."

"I think I'll be sad to leave the Netherwhere, Da." Otter hugged Tanner and then hugged the captain.

"Well, of course you will be," Captain Maul said. "But you know, my daughter's a dragon, so could bring us here again in a blink."

Otter's eyes widened.

"Couldn't be telling you that, though; now, could I?" The captain tugged on his beard braids. "Last time she did that— when was it, Tan?"

"Fifth birthday, mad as a frog in a jug that we wouldn't let her chase kelpies." Tanner laughed. "Then the chimera—"

"Why didn't you tell me you know Ebba?" Otter asked.

"We thought about it, but . . ." one father started.

"How do you explain a grumpy chimera with lion, goat, and snake heads?" her other father continued.

"Right, then," Otter said. "I'll chase the kids onto the ship."

"Ottilie?" the captain called. When she paused, he said, "When you have a chance, scritch your mum right at the eye ridge. You liked that as a wee lizard."

"Was I dragon shaped for long when you got me?" she asked. "Shouldn't I remember?"

"Nah. You were mostly baby-human shaped, but sometimes you'd launch yourself into the sea, and then there you were, scales and snout," Tanner said.

"Cutest little snout," the captain muttered. "Nearly broke my heart to tell you not to swim in the sea anymore. It wasn't safe, though. Your mum . . ."

"Worried," Tanner finished.

"Do you remember when she had that cold and kept setting the mattress on fire?" the captain asked with a guffaw.

Her fathers grinned at each other, reminiscing in the way of adults over Otter's childhood . . . as a reptile.

She walked away from them a little faster than she normally would, as she wasn't *quite* ready to listen to stories of her cute snout.

By evening, the ship was loaded, including barrels of water and some fruit and salted fish that the Lost Ones donated as payment for safe passage for their departing members—even though the captain said it wasn't necessary.

"Hey there!" Otter yelled. "If you're coming aboard, get aboard."

Ten of the Lost Ones scuttled toward the *Tempest*. Most of them wanted to go home to their thief houses in Glass City, but two were hoping to find their missing families and one was hoping to live on a ship.

"Tethers," Tanner called a few minutes later as he stomped across the deck.

"All hands!" the captain bellowed.

Both fathers and Marian—tall and alert in the water—watched Otter for the order to depart.

Otter nodded to Marian and then looked at her fathers and yelled, "Prepare to set sail!"

"Into the sea!" Marian's voice boomed as she led the *Tempest* out of the shallow part of the sea with the speed of kelpies on a hunt.

Then there was a waterfall, and the dragon shot straight up the center of it until the ship was in the eye of the Maelstrom.

"Steady on, lad," one of the crew said to London, who was looking a bit green again. He made an "all's fine" gesture to reassure Otter that he had the stomach to be a sailor.

Finally, the *Tempest* burst out of the twisty tunnel and landed with a lurch in the much calmer waters on the edge of the Crimson Sea. Overhead, the moon hung in the sky like it had the day they left, and kelpies sliced the waves with hooves sharp as a fresh blade. Everything was the same, but it all seemed different now that Otter knew she was a dragon.

"Get the Lost Ones settled . . . ?" the captain ask-ordered her and London.

They led the ten kids to the hold of the ship.

"That section is the calmest." London pointed. "I slept down here when I was a stowaway."

The kids looked at him curiously.

"But nowhere's safe from rocking when there's a storm. I puked for days when we hit one," he added. "It passes."

Otter rolled her eyes. "Not everyone gets seasick. Most of you—maybe all of you—*won't* get sick."

London shook his head and made a gagging gesture while

he clutched his belly, making the kids laugh. Otter could see that he was far more at ease with kids than she'd ever felt.

Because you're not really a kid, she thought.

"I'm going to take a watch now," London announced as he headed up the stairs. "I'll be back down when it's my turn to sleep."

Otter observed the ragtag group of wholly human kids. Each one had crudely woven bags made from some sort of Netherwhere plant and stuffed with snacks and blankets. Honestly, they were better provisioned than some of the crew was when they'd signed on to the *Tempest*.

Otter wasn't surprised to see that some of them seemed nervous as they picked out spots and set up beds, and she made plans to show them why the sea was wondrous. But first, she decided the best thing was to stay here with them. She went and grabbed herself a blanket, which was woven of dragon hide. Then she stretched out at the bottom of the steps so she would notice any comings or goings.

Mostly it was about making them feel safe, but they were also armed strangers. Being a kid didn't make a person harmless, and these were children who'd faced dragons and adults. Every last one of them had carried a spear on board. Her fathers had allowed it, but Otter wasn't about to let anyone roam the *Tempest* with a spear.

As she was about to go asleep, she heard London call down from above, "Good night, Flames."

Otter grumbled, but she was smiling as she fell asleep in the hold with the kids.

SOMETIME LATER, OTTER woke to London shaking her. She looked at him, and he held a finger to his lips.

"Black sails," he whispered. "I went up the mast to the sit and think, and I could see the sails. Two ships. East and southeast."

"*Here?*" she whispered.

"Yes. Speeding toward us, flying the black sails," London confirmed.

Otter let her mind drop under the sea's surface and feel for any dragons. "Stay away!" she warned them.

Then she told London, "We're usually faster than anything out here. The *Tempie* outruns every ship in existence . . . but that's partly because we usually have dragons leading us. Tonight, we're on our own, so we'll be slower."

"Speed doesn't matter tonight, anyhow. This is an *ambush*, not a race," London said. "The pirates are using a thieves' trick. One thief approaches from the front while the other comes up behind the mark. No way out. And that's just the two ships I saw. Let's hope there aren't more!"

Several of the kids woke while they were talking, and they were already gathering spears.

"I'll alert the captain and night crew," London said, and disappeared up the steps.

Otter looked at the kids, who were all awake now. "You can stay down here."

"You don't hunt; you don't eat," one said. "We will help."

"Not a—"

"They sink the ship, and we're out of luck," another said.

"Let's go, then. And when we get up top, keep low in case they have spyglasses," Otter instructed.

Crouching down so they didn't attract attention, Otter and the ten former Lost Ones crept up to the deck, hoping they were prepared for what they might find.

CHAPTER 19

London

London sat on deck with the children. One by one, every lantern on the ship was put out. The only light came from the sliver of moon and the glow from the decks of the approaching ships. The pirates' ships were brightly lit, making sure to be seen—and the lights directed their intended victims' gazes to their tattered black flags.

"Stay put," one of the older men of the *Tempest* said, eyeing the kids and their spears. "I don't want anyone stabbed by accident."

London waited, watching black sails flap in the wind. He had no idea how close the pirates were. He had learned earlier, when watching kelpies dance and whales breach, that distances at sea were tricky. He'd think the creatures were near enough to touch, but then the ship sailed and sailed and still didn't reach them.

"Do you think they're ghost ships?" one of the kids asked in a loud whisper of onion-scented breath.

London tried to bat away the scent as he asked, "Ghost ships?"

"Our last ship was a ghost," another kid said. "After the dragon smashed into it, the crew was gone, and the ship bobbed off."

"A couple kids stayed on it when we started to sink, and one was a ward worker. Plugged the hole," another added. "So instead of falling in the sea, we could stay on the ship. After the dragons explained that we could go to the Netherwhere, the ship sailed on. No people. Just a ghost ship. Good magic."

"Right," London said. "I hope these two are filled with ghosts or kids, but . . ."

No one answered because, obviously, the odds were that the pirate ships with their full sails were crewed by actual pirates. London hoped that his seafaring life wasn't about to be cut short. He had no desire to join a pirate crew or end up "in the drink" with kelpies. He felt loads better about the dragons, but the kelpies were still meat eaters, and children were, of course, made of meat.

He must have dozed, because the next thing London knew, he startled awake as a cannonball sizzled overhead. Then came another and another.

London sat up as the glowing ball of metal collided with the sail and, in a moment of unexpected reaction, *bounced* back and plopped into the sea.

He rubbed his eyes.

Flaming balls ought not bounce off cloth. But then he

remembered the sails on the *Tempest* were now made of skin that a dragon had shed.

"Flame resistant!" London exclaimed. "Thank you, Marian and the slugs!"

Likewise, the slime-coated planks seemed to repel the fiery hot balls that thudded onto the sides of the ship. The Netherwhere repairs had been even more incredible than he'd realized!

"All hands, keep cover!" Captain Maul shouted.

"And stay away from the railings!" Tanner added. "Can't see to fish you out, iffen you go over."

Sparks rained down from the mast where the flaming cannonball had singed the wood. They were like tiny fireflies lighting up the darkened ship—and it *was* darkened. All the lanterns were tamped down, so in the great expanse of sea, the H.M.S. *Tempest* was all but hidden. The pirates, though, had obviously already fixed the *Tempest* in their cannon sights—or they had a ward worker on ship.

"Do you want to see them?" the boy with the onion breath asked. "I can draw a ward for you to see them in the dark. I can't do everyone, but . . ."

"Yes. Thank you . . . What's your name?"

"I'm Bertrand. You can call me Berty," the boy said.

London felt a strange sensation. It was as if another lens, something wet and cold, had slid across his eye. The ward worked, though. He could see the shapes of the crew.

London looked at Berty, noticing now that the boy was thin

and cautious-looking. He would've made a good thief, with his darting movements and observant stance.

"Well done," London said. "You need to do that ward for Captain Maul and the first mate, Tanner, and . . . How many people can you do?"

"Maybe six?"

"Six is good. Come with me." London crept with Berty along the deck, close enough to the rail not to bump into anyone. As he went, he murmured, over and over, "London here. Not an attacker."

The crew, even though they couldn't see much, tensed as he passed. Maybe they heard him, or maybe they just felt the brush of his jacket. London wasn't sure, but he crept onward until he reached the captain at the helm of the ship.

"Ward worker with me, Captain Maul," London said. "Called Berty. He did something and made me see in the dark."

"Do it." The captain didn't hesitate about trying the unknown magic. "They won't expect us to have the advantage of carrying a ward worker. Most cargo ships are defenseless against pirates."

Tanner snorted. "*Most* ships don't sail into dragon-infested waters, either."

As Berty worked his magic on the captain, flaming cannonballs continued to shoot overhead.

"Do Tan's eyes next so we can watch to see if any enemies are trying to sneak up on us," the captain ordered.

London stood there, more afraid than he wanted to admit. Once both men were able to see, London asked, "What do we do?"

The captain and first mate exchanged looks. Then they both said, "We fight, lad."

London nodded. "*Most* ships would simply try to flee."

Tanner's hand clapped London's shoulder. "But we're not most ships, now, are we?"

CHAPTER 20

· — ◆ — ◆ — ◆ — ·

Sofia

S ofia was unsure that she'd been delivered to the right place. The bedroom was immense! At least thirty kids could sleep on the fancy rugs that covered the marble and wood floors. Green vines had been painted on the walls, and the wooden bed was covered with a bright floral bedspread. The fireplace was blazing.

"Am I to wait here?" she asked the Raven.

"Wait, read, nap," the woman replied with a shrug. "Whatever you like."

Testing the rules, Sofia asked, "Could I leave?"

The guard smiled. "Queen says you are to advise her. You can't do that if you leave."

So the beautiful room might, in fact, also be a prison. Sofia nodded. She was tired in a way that didn't make sense. It wasn't as if she'd been lifting trinkets in the streets. She'd simply met with the queen. She smothered a yawn.

The Raven watched Sofia and softened briefly, like

someone had let her strings slacken. "Takes a rare person to be bold enough to confront the queen. Now rest, sister of Merry. Things can get busy in the palace."

Once the guard left, Sofia immediately tried the door. *Locked.* And the window. *Covered in bars.* There wasn't any need to leave, but after a few years of living on the streets, bars and locks felt like danger.

The room was warm, though, and there was a bookshelf taller than Sofia. She walked over to it, scanning the titles. Before she touched any of them, she wiped her hands on her skirt to make sure they were clean. Then she curled up on a chair with a book.

She wasn't careless enough to put her back to the door, but she relaxed enough to be startled a while later when there was a knock at the door—followed by a woman dropping off a heavy tray of food.

Sofia looked at the heaping tray with wide eyes. A whole potato bigger than her fist, a leg of meat, a bowl of something green and leafy that looked like weeds, and a jug of cold milk. As if that wasn't enough, there were tea, honey, several pastries, and a chunk of bread.

Who ate that much at midday?

Once she was alone again, Sofia took the cloth napkin and wrapped the bread, some pastries, and half the potato for later. Food was everything on the street. Even the cold wasn't so bad when your belly was full.

The serving woman returned to take her tray away and, before leaving, commented, "Good appetite, then. But not fond of salad?"

So that's what those green weeds in the bowl were called!

Sofia yawned and noticed the bed. It looked like a cloud, puffy and huge, and Sofia had never seen such a thing. There was even a little stool to climb up! Sofia ignored the stool and took a running leap onto the cloudlike bed.

It was even softer than it looked.

Sofia closed her eyes and must have drowsed, because suddenly a Raven was there, and Sofia was being brought back to the queen.

THE QUEEN INTRODUCED Sofia to two of her advisors, who bowed to Sofia as if she was their equal.

The alchemist, Master Nightshade, had a disheveled look, as if he had no time to bother with appearances. Every thief had heard of him; he collected thieves and took them to his country estate, where they could help at his manor and earn money of their own.

Sofia gave him a smile.

The alchemist grinned widely, as if he'd been expecting something unpleasant but was presented with a happy surprise instead.

"The girl looks like Merry, but she's definitely *not*," Nightshade pronounced. "Merry doesn't smile like that unless she stole something."

"Yes, it wasn't too hard to notice the difference," the queen said as she looked at the one called Meister Tik, the sword master. Sofia thought the queen might have rolled her eyes.

Surely, a *queen* wouldn't do that!

"Meet Sofia. Sister of Merry Ward," Queen Evangeline announced. "My new advisor on the matter of thief houses and an alarming report on relocation ships stealing children from the streets of my city!"

The men seemed as surprised as the queen had been by the news of child snatchers.

"We must find out who's paying them," the queen said. "Track the money, and you'll find the reason."

Meister Tik nodded. "I'll have someone trustworthy investigate, Your Majesty."

"Good. And I've already sent Ravens to the dock to stop any more such attempts. The nerve of people, stealing *my* citizens. And children at that!"

The queen looked angry enough to bite someone, and that was when Florie arrived at the Glass Palace, brought in by more of the queen's guards.

Sofia saw the strain in Florie's expression, and she wanted to tell him the queen's scowl wasn't because of him.

"*Not* helpful." Florie turned to look up at the guard who tried to push Florie's chair. "If I need help, I'll let you know. How do you think I get through my days? If you really want to help, fix some baskets of food to take home to my family. A few blankets wouldn't go amiss, either."

Then he straightened his jacket and grinned at Sofia. "Meredith."

"Florence!" Sofia curtsied to him. Then she turned to the queen. "Your Majesty, gentlemen, may I present Florence, founder and representative of the House of Florence."

She'd practiced the words in her head, and as she said them, the queen smiled in approval.

Florie bent at the waist, bowing as was custom before the queen. "Your Majesty."

"Florence, may I introduce Queen Evangeline and Meister Tik, headmaster of the Corvus School for the Artfully Inclined." Sofia gestured at the heavily armed man with the braid and then the alchemist. "And the Queen's Alchemist, Master Nightshade."

The alchemist looked up. "Pleasure to see you, Florie. I've taken in quite a few lads from your house."

"Trained them up and sent them into the world with skills," Florie said. "Appreciate it."

Nightshade shrugged. "I do what I can in the memory of an old friend who was once an orphan, too."

"Merry has spoken often of the underground, but *Sofia*"—the queen gestured—"spoke of you in particular, Florence."

Florie's expression was blank. "Who?"

"The girl you sent to deceive me," the queen continued, motioning to Sofia. "Meredith's twin, I wager."

"I'm not sure who Sofia is . . ." he said.

The queen scoffed. "Why are children always so impertinent?"

"Because we raise ourselves?" Florie said dryly.

The queen let out a long sigh. "Go on, then. Out with it. Your plan to get an emissary to my door worked. You have my attention, Florence. You obviously have important thoughts to share if you'd risk *Sofia's* safety—"

"If Your Royal Majesty would look after the children of Glass City, I wouldn't have had to attempt a ruse." Florie scowled. "*I* take care of them. *I* feed them. *I* clothe them. What have *you* done for the children of Glass City?"

The queen said nothing, and Sofia saw the sword master's hand fall to the hilt of his blade. But then the alchemist started laughing.

"Nightshade," the queen started. "Manners, please."

"He's so bold. I like it," Master Nightshade said. "Not *quite* as rude as some, but not everyone can be as contentious as Meredith . . . or the heir."

"Or your son," the sword master muttered.

"Daring young people, my queen." Master Nightshade was no longer laughing but instead sounded serious and wise. "They are fierce. Ready to fight for change. That bravery is a kind of magic all its own." Nightshade motioned to Florie. "He sits in front of you, armed with words and ideas, ready to slay the Glass Queen for the children under his wings."

"I wasn't—" Florie started.

"He's not here to hurt you, Your Majesty. Neither of us are!" Sofia quickly said. "I swear to you! No slaying!"

"I know, child." The queen nodded. "Nightshade simply has an intolerable way with words."

"You could do worse than this one in future advisors." Nightshade pointed at Florie. "He has plans. Thieves always do."

"Tik?" the queen asked.

"His house has a good reputation," Meister Tik said. "As do House Jerusalem and House Sydney."

Sofia and Florie exchanged a look.

"Meredith has been bringing a lot of knowledge to me. We *were* working on a plan to approach the thieves' houses, but obviously not fast enough," the queen said. "We have people looking at locations for orphanages and schools. Merry has been worse than a dragonet, buzzing about with updates and requests."

"Oh." Sofia folded her hands together.

"Your sister is a lot like you, Sofia."

Sofia wasn't sure what to say to that. She just hoped she would find out soon if it was true.

The queen motioned to Meister Tik and Master Nightshade. "I trust these men above all others, and I give you my word that we *will* move faster now. And in the meantime, they will see to whatever the House of Florence needs while we plan a future."

"With our input!" Florie added.

"Yes, yes, with your input," the queen agreed.

"I'm eager to meet the young thieves, Florie," said Master Nightshade. "I could take about twenty if they'd like."

Florie nodded.

"And Corvus has room for at least twenty, maybe up to fifty if we open the new Wardrop dormitory ahead of schedule," Meister Tik said. "However, I will only take those seeking to be a Raven. Corvus has a mission. I won't ignore the mission."

"Up to fifty what?" Sofia finally asked.

"Thieves," Florie said.

"*What?*" Sofia asked. "What are you talking about? Take them where?"

"To where they'll have a future, and safety," Meister Tik said. "You wanted food and warmth—an education . . ."

Sofia felt as if her head was spinning. "Truly?"

"Yes," the queen said. "We will make it happen."

"There's a lot to figure out." Florie turned to Sofia. "And I'll be here working with them on the plans."

"But if you're *here*, who's going to talk to the kids at home?"

"*You* are, Sofia," Florie suggested.

Sofia nodded. She'd be happy to go talk to the thieves. She didn't want to sit around talking to adults anymore. *Someone* had to return to talk to the rest of the House of Florence, and it might as well be her.

Sofia put on her cloak and got ready to leave. "Wait, what if not everyone wants to leave the underground?"

"That'll be okay," Florie said. "We can figure out a way to make life better there, too."

Florie followed her to the doorway, and before she left, Sofia leaned over and hugged him. It wasn't what thieves did, but this was a special day. "They are truly listening!" she whispered.

Florie's arms went around her in a protective squeeze. "Thanks to you, Sofia. You got this started. Well done!"

"Not *just* me!" Sofia said as she reached in her cloak pocket and pulled out one of the little pastries she'd hidden away earlier during her midday meal. "Before I forget, you have to taste this."

Florie took a bite of the pastry, and his face lit up. "Delicious. I'm going to ask for more of these. Schools. Warm homes. Medicine. Pastries. Things *will* get better for us!"

CHAPTER 21

◆————◆————◆

Otter

Unlike most of the crew—who were all stumbling and fumbling along—Otter had always seen as well in the dark as in the light. Now, as she searched the deck for intruders, she wondered if her sight was a dragon thing, but she didn't wonder long. A loud boom echoed.

"Steady!" one of the crew members called as another cannonball sizzled overhead. Fortunately, the Netherwhere repairs were holding up.

It wasn't the first time the *Tempest* had seen pirates, but the pirates had never targeted them. Nothing about the *Tempest* was interesting enough to make them a focus. Just an average, slightly worn tall ship. Not as big as most. Otter's father let it be known that they carried simple cargo, low-dollar items, and that they barely made any profit.

What pirate would want *that*?

Either their ruse was up, or these pirates were desperate. Either way, it was trouble.

As she finished the loop around the deck, Otter called out, "Clear."

In the shadows, she could see the crew relax, shoulders loosen and sword hands unclench. They could all fight—every sailor had to know swordfighting—but it didn't mean they wanted to do so.

"And the seas?" one of the men asked. "Any scales?"

"None. I warned them." Otter smiled, though he couldn't see her. The crew cared a great deal for the "big lizards," even though the creatures had nearly killed them more than a few times.

"Ottilie!" Da called out, looking around to find her.

"Here!" She made her way to him, surprised when he looked directly at her. "Da?"

"Wards." He nodded to one of the Lost Ones. "The urchin fixed me and Tan."

"And me," London said.

"So only a few of us on the ship can see." Otter thought about it. They could steer, watch for invaders, fight a bit, but none of that helped with the cannonballs.

"We need to get to land," the captain said. "Warn Her Majesty that there are pirates in her seas."

Her seas? Otter looked at the water. Weren't these the *dragons'* seas?

Another cannonball whizzed through the air. This one hit part of the starboard railing.

"I'll ask a few dragonets to go tell her we're under attack," Otter offered, already sending messages to them.

"The parts the slugs didn't slime aren't protected," London said, pointing at a small fire that several crewmembers were dousing.

"That's bad. We need to stay dark and sail slowly," Tanner suggested. "Head toward Glass City."

"Or we could skirt back into the Maelstrom?" Otter suggested.

Her fathers both glanced at her.

The captain said, "Ebba's not always that friendly to adults."

"That was friendly?" Otter asked.

"And if Marian and the others come, they'll need to sink the lot of the pirates. The danger to them, to the queen, to us if word of dragons got out . . ." Tanner said with a shudder.

"Do we have a cannon?" London asked.

"The *Tempest* is not a pirate vessel, lad," Tanner grumbled. "We have harpoons, nets, the anchor, and . . . some frogs."

"Frogs?" London asked.

Otter's fathers said nothing, so she told London, "The cargo. The barrels are full of frogs."

"Frogs," London repeated again. "What *kind* of frogs?"

"Itty-bitty poisonous ones," Captain Maul said. "We were delivering them up north. They use the goo on them for their weapons."

Otter and London exchanged a look. She knew that they were thinking the same thing when London said, "We need to get the poisonous frogs onto the enemy ship."

Tanner sighed. "The cargo wasn't fated to make it to delivery, was it?"

The captain grinned. "Burning welts if you touch the slimy little things. Better those barrels spill on the pirates' decks than ours."

"If we crack the lid of the barrel and launch it onto the deck . . ." Otter considered. "We need a grappling hook, a barrel of frogs, and a dinghy."

Her fathers looked wary. "You, Ottilie Jo Maul, aren't going off to risk your neck."

"Well, I am," London said. "I can see, and I'm fast."

"I can see, too," Tanner said. "Cap'n stays on the ship."

"And if there's a fight, which of us is most useful on ship? You or me?" London asked.

Otter scowled. *Her* plan. *Her* ship. *Her* fathers. *Her* friend. And they weren't listening to her. "Dragon," she said loudly.

"Where?" Tanner asked.

Otter pointed at herself. "Right here."

"Now, Ottilie—"

"Dragon. I'm a dragon. Not some wee helpless thing," she snapped at them. "I should be on the dinghy. I can swim better than any of you."

When no one replied, she nodded once.

"I'll join you," London insisted.

"Great. Two ships, two dinghies. We'll each take one." She folded her arms. "Now, we need a few volunteers."

Various voices piped up.

"Here!"

"Me!"

"I'll go."

Ten voices. All the Lost Ones had volunteered. She had her crew.

"Right, then. All ten of you are coming! I'll get the *adult* crew to bring up a few barrels and ready the two dinghies."

No one said another word of objection as she walked away.

WHEN OTTER RETURNED to the main deck, she found the ten kids, each with a small barrel of frogs. Tanner was with them. He had giant gloves that stretched up to his armpits, and a face shield strapped down from ear to ear and chin to hair. He nodded at the smaller barrels and said, "Put the hopping monsters into tiny water barrels. Easier to hoist."

"Thank you," Otter said.

He reached out like he was going to pat her head, but grimaced as he, apparently, realized he was wearing a glove coated in poisonous slime.

London gave Otter a wide smile, and she couldn't help returning it.

"You'll be silent," Captain Maul ordered.

"Like a dragon," Otter promised, staring up at her father. "Quiet and quick."

"A *cautious* dragon," he grumbled.

Each of the children quickly strapped their barrel onto their back so they'd have free hands when they climbed. Typically, the barrels were used to gather fresh water on one of the uninhabited islands at sea. They'd need new barrels after this—but better that than needing a new ship!

The crew of the *Tempest* lowered the dinghies, and Otter

climbed down the ladder. Once she was in it, steady and able to help her crew of five kids, the kids shimmied down the ladder and got into the tiny boat.

She watched as London descended and helped his crew. And then they were off! At this hour, the water looked like black ink on this near-moonless night, magical but deadly.

The two dinghies separated and began to row in opposite directions. One dinghy headed toward each pirate ship.

No one spoke, so the only sound was the swish of oars. Voices carried over water, and they were audible for longer distances than seemed reasonable.

Otter was betting that the crew of the pirate ship—at least those on watch—were scanning for sails, for a massive ship, for the *Tempest* fleeing. They were, in the way of sailors on watch, staring out into the distance, not straight *down*.

At least that was Otter's hope. A cannonball to a dinghy would be disastrous.

The kids rowed and rowed until they were right up alongside one of the enemy ships—the *Morrigan*.

Otter mouthed, "Chain." The kids flung the grappling hooks upward. The soft clunks seemed loud, but no pirates came to investigate.

A few kids steadied the dinghy as the ladder was attached to the side of the ship, then Otter and Berty scurried up and down the ladder until all five barrels were on the main deck of the *Morrigan*.

Finally, Otter ascended the ladder for the last time. This was the trickiest part! Carefully, she pulled the corks out of all five barrels and quickly set them rolling across the deck.

The rainbow-hued frogs, shaken on the trip, were like a multicolored explosion on the far side of the deck. Otter watched them escape as she descended the ladder.

As long as no one saw the kids, they'd be long gone before the pirates even noticed their poisonous invaders.

Otter and the kids rowed away as quickly and quietly as they could. By the time they were well away from the *Morrigan*, the shouts of enraged pirates broke out.

"Vermin!"

Yells of pain rang out.

"Grab it!"

"Toss those devils overboard!"

More cries of pain as foolish pirates tried to grab hopping poisonous frogs. Each touch would leave a welt. It probably wouldn't *kill* anyone, but it would keep them busy enough that the *Tempest* could flee to safer shores while the enemies were busy with slime-coated invaders.

The kids were grinning, but they stayed silent as they continued to row back toward the *Tempest*.

But the smile of victory was wiped off Otter's face when she heard shouts coming from the other pirate ship.

With her night vision, she could see that London and his crew were done delivering the frogs, but now one of the pirates was leaning down, aiming to shoot an arrow with a flaming tip toward London's dinghy.

"No," she whispered. Yelling wasn't an option unless they wanted to be a target, too.

London and the kids with him were illuminated briefly by flames.

She watched helplessly as they tried to douse the flames. Even that was too slow; the fire had allowed one of the pirates to aim a cannon. As Otter looked on, a small cannonball hit the tiny craft, shattering the floor of it. Screams and yells rose from their tiny boat.

"London!" Otter cried out as she saw the dinghy sink.

Without another thought, she flung herself overboard and started to swim toward the sinking kids.

Faster! she thought. *I need to go faster! What if they can't swim? What if there are kelpies?*

She surged forward.

They are mine! she thought to any kelpies or anything else lurking in the water.

When she saw the kids, she swam under them so they would all be on her back and . . . Otter paused. Why was she suddenly big enough to fit five kids her same size on top of her back? Why was she so fast? What had happened?

Otter flexed her arms, noticing the way the water moved and how very small the other kids looked.

Then she flapped her wings, using them like massive oars, and realized she was an actual full-sized *dragon*.

CHAPTER 22

◆———◆———◆

London

London let out an embarrassing noise as the cannonball hit the dinghy. Luckily, none of the kids were in the direct line of fire, but they'd all been thrown back by its force.

"We're sunk!" one of the children yelled.

"Again!" another added.

And they were. The tiny boat was destroyed. They were all afloat—six kids clutching planks from their sunken boat.

"Paddle," London urged. "Stay together and paddle."

They were so far from the *Tempest* that London wasn't convinced that they'd make it, but he wasn't about to say that. No thief worth his salt was going to admit fatigue. A thief did the work but didn't complain. In many ways, London thought it was good training for a life at sea—a life he wouldn't get if they didn't get back to the *Tempest*.

He paddled and listened, but it wasn't a cannonball he heard. There was some creature in the water. He could feel the current from it surging toward him. It was huge, bigger than a kelpie.

Where was Otter when you needed her?

"Faster, mates!" He hoped they didn't notice the beast advancing. "Come on, now. Paddle!" His voice cracked as the creature brushed against his leg.

"What's under us?" another kid asked.

"Nothing. Just paddle!" London thought lying was daft. They could feel it, too, but he couldn't bring himself to admit a monster was that near.

It surged up out of the water, gleaming scales the size of platters. The thing shimmered like an opal had been hammered flat. But any awe he felt suddenly died because it opened its mouth. A row of sharp teeth, fish catchers, lined the front of its mouth. In the back, London saw crushing, grinding teeth.

Was the dragon going to rip him apart and grind his bones? Otter was off on the other dinghy; otherwise she could talk to it. Was it better to call to her? Or would that expose her location to the pirates, too?

London clutched the wreckage of the dinghy with one arm, and with the other, he pulled his fist back and punched the dragon in the eye.

"Paddle!" he yelled.

Then the dragon's maw snapped shut, scraping his face, and he was inside the mouth of a dragon! He stood on the creature's tongue, which was a sort of gross that he couldn't even fathom—and he'd waded through Blood Close in Glass City and worked in an alchemist's lab cleaning experiments gone wrong.

It's going to swallow me whole!

But it didn't tear or crush him. Instead, the dragon was *swimming*.

London wrapped his arms around the tip of a long tooth. The edges scraped his arms, and he started to bleed. But he was not going to be swallowed by a giant carnivorous beast!

As the creature swam, none of the other kids joined him in the mouth. That, at least, was a relief. After several moments, it stopped, and London braced himself. But all that happened was the mouth finally opened.

London jumped out—right onto the deck of the *Tempest*.

He looked as the other five kids from his sunken dinghy slid off the dragon's neck. They seemed perfectly calm.

"Not our first dragon ride," one said smugly as London stared at the dragon.

"You weren't trying to eat me?" London asked.

The creature snorted.

"Are you okay?" Tanner said, rushing up to . . . the dragon.

And London felt foolish. Surely, it wasn't . . . *Otter*. She was on the other boat. And she had said she didn't know *how* to be dragon shaped!

Then the captain stomped over and stared at the dragon that was mostly in the sea but partly on ship. "Ottilie, come on. You can't stay that way."

Tanner patted the creature's scaled neck. "Come on. You must be sleepy." He glanced at the captain. "Lass always did need a nap after a swim."

London's mouth gaped open. He stared at the dragon. And then the air felt all tingly, like right before a storm, when everything feels like it might spark, and there stood a scowling girl.

She glared at him. "Next time I'll let the kelpies eat you, yeah?"

"Otter—"

"And I have blood in my . . ." Her words trailed off, and she grimaced before adding, "You got blood on my teeth."

"Because you *bit me*!" he yelled.

Then she spun and stomped off, even as the other kids were all thanking her. The captain went with her.

"You did a good job, lad," Tanner said, patting his back. "The enemy's not firing, and the ship's lights are all on. We're clear to sail."

London looked. In the gleam of the *Barnacle*'s lanterns, he could see people flapping their arms and leaping around, looking rather like enormous angry faeries. The frogs mightn't have been fast enough to prevent the almost drowning of London's small crew, but they were clearly doing the necessary work now.

"Only got the one cannon fired," Tanner said. "Sheer bad luck that they got you."

Still watching the silhouettes of leaping pirates, London said, "She bit me."

"It's not venomous," one of the passing crew members said. "When she was teething, that little beast nipped everyone. Got me right on the, er, posterior one day."

London nodded. He was glad Otter had saved him, but he couldn't quite make his mind accept that Otter was, indeed, a giant dragon. He had *thought* it made sense, but then, well, he was standing in her *mouth* getting cut on gigantic dragon teeth.

He was currently soaked in dragon spit.

"We'll head back to the city," Tanner told him. "If you want to go to Northland, you can catch our ride out, but if you want to stay in Glass City, no one will think less of you."

"Go back?"

"Queen needs to know about the pirates," Tanner explained. "Too close to the dragons. And we can't keep the kids all on the *Tempest*, now, can we?"

London nodded again. *Did* he want to go back to the city? Or to Northland?

"Think about it," Tanner stressed. "Life at sea is fraught with peril. Usually not this much, mind you, but dragon hunting isn't for the easily daunted."

"Neither is the life of a thief." London watched Tanner walk away, and then he went to the railing. He was wet, smelled of sea and spit, and had been nearly drowned, sunken, and fallen through the Maelstrom. He'd faced dragons, an armed horde of lost children, a chimera, faeries, dragonets, and pirates.

London stared out at the dark water. Without any light, it looked like an entirely different thing than the gleaming sea that he watched when the daylight shined down on it. He thought of that moment when he didn't realize that Otter was the strange unseen beast under him in the dark, deep water. Then he thought about the pirates firing at the ship, sinking the dinghy and, before that, setting it on fire. London remembered the storm when he was hiding and the dragon attack when he was tethered to the ship.

And he smiled.

By the time the ship headed toward Glass City, London was absolutely sure that it didn't matter what land it was, he wouldn't be as happy on any land as he was at sea.

"Sign me up," London told Captain Maul when the man returned to deck to check the status of pending pirate attacks.

"Sign you up for . . . ?"

"Whatever job you have open." London crossed his arms, hoping that the captain wasn't going to refuse.

Then Tanner and Otter joined the captain, just as London added, "I want to be at sea, sir. And I'd like to be on the *Tempest*."

Tanner and Captain Maul exchanged a look. Then the captain said, "We fall through the Maelstrom, nearly get sunk by a dragon, are beset by pirates, and you *want to sign on*?"

London nodded. "I do."

"Did he hit his head? Swallow too much sea?" Tanner asked, but he looked like he was fighting a smile.

"Seawater's good. It helped with the frog burns." London held out his arm, where four or five bright-green raised bumps stood out.

"You got *burned*?" Otter poked him. "You were to dump them on the pirate ship, not—"

"I'm okay." London shrugged. "They didn't all hop away from the barrel. A couple liked me, I guess?"

Otter opened her mouth to say something else, but before she could, the captain asked, "What makes you want to be on *this* ship?"

"My best friend's here." London glanced at Otter. "Scales and all, I'm betting there's no one else quite like you. You're like I thought having a sister would be. I want to be here because *you're* here, Otter."

Otter finally looked at him. "Sorry I bit you a little. I was scared you'd get eaten by kelpies."

"Nope. Just a protective dragon. The scar will make me look like a sailor, though." London reached out to hug her, and this time she let him. Quietly, he whispered, "It's okay. Honest! You didn't mean to bite me. Sorry I punched your eye."

Tanner cleared his throat loudly. "Captain, what say you?"

Captain Maul scratched his chin braids. "Fine. I suppose we can stand having two kids. Least this one won't need nappies." He reached out and tugged both kids into a hug. "Welcome to the family, London T. Maul."

And London felt a warm feeling that he couldn't quite explain. He had a surname, and not one but *two* parents, and a sister.

"Welcome home," his sister, the dragon, said. Then she smiled and added, "Brother."

CHAPTER 23

◆———◆———◆

Sofia

Before being escorted out of the palace, Sofia had to make way for a group of Ravens arriving with a message for the queen.

One of those Ravens—a man with a shaved head—had a dragonet perched on each shoulder. It was a rare thing to bond with the tiny dragons, but Sofia wasn't surprised. The queen's guards were a rare sort.

The one that walked Sofia out joked with her, "So, what shall I call you, if you are not Lady Light-Fingers?"

"Miss Sofia?" she offered—and then she stole a ring for giggles.

The guard bowed to her at the gate, and Sofia said, "You dropped this . . ."

As Sofia tossed the ring to the guard, they shared a smile. She might not be the infamous Merry Ward, but she felt like she was now walking taller than she had only yesterday.

She was marveling over the fact that she had gained the

queen's and Florie's trust—*and* she'd made a difference, when she heard a girl's voice call out, "It's *you*!"

Sofia looked up to see the girl she hadn't stopped thinking about staring back at her.

"Merry Ward!" Sofia said. "Hi, I'm . . ." Her words faded because she wasn't sure what to say.

There were a few other kids with Merry, and they all looked as stunned as Sofia felt, but nothing else could have shocked her as much as Merry's next words.

"My sister. I knew it!" Merry whispered. "You're my sister, but I thought . . . They said you were *dead*."

Sofia stood there in awe. This was her sister, her twin. "I thought I dreamed you. They told me you were imaginary, said you weren't real . . ."

"Pfff. Real enough to steal a future for myself," Merry said.

"Yeah? Me too." Sofia stepped a little closer.

"I went back to try to find you . . . just to check if they lied," Merry said. "But our old house was gone."

"I was probably already living in Florie's house by then," Sofia answered.

"And now? What are you doing here?" Merry asked.

Neither Merry nor the others said a word while Sofia explained about living at Florie's, about all that had happened with the queen—and that Queen Evangeline had agreed to move faster to help.

"*Really?*" Merry said. "How did you manage that? I've tried, but . . ."

"It wasn't just me. I pretended to be you, and then Florie

met with her . . . I think things are really going to start to change!"

"You'll have to tell me more when we have more time, just the two of us." Merry spoke quickly. "And now that we've found each other, we have to be together, right? You . . . you ought to come to Corvus and live with me. Will you? Please?"

Sofia nodded yes, and Merry kept talking. "We'll figure out which house you'll be in, but I think no matter what, you ought to stay in the wing where I live. I stay near Vicky." Merry looked at one of the girls with her. "This is Vicky. Oh, there's so much to tell you. But wait, what name are you using?"

"Sofia."

"*Sofia* Ward," Merry said. "I think it works. You?"

Sofia nodded. "I like that."

They didn't hug or anything. Sofia considered it for a moment, but her sister—her *twin sister!*—carried on talking, so Sofia figured that was what they were meant to do.

"So Vicky—Victoria Wardrop—is the queen's heir. The princess, I guess, is what you ought to call her, but she's my job. Taking care of her. And this is Nightshade, younger alchemist." Merry pointed. "And this is Milan. Do you know him from—"

"Oh, for goodness' sake," the princess interrupted. "*Hug* her, Merry. I hug my sisters. Nightshade hugs his brother. Just hug her!"

And Sofia stepped forward as her sister did, and for the first time she could remember, she hugged her sister. The girl from her dreams was here, real, and they were together again. They could figure the rest out later.

Merry hugged Sofia back with a hard squeeze that made her sure that Merry was happy, too.

"Hello, sister," Merry said.

"Hello, sister," Sofia answered. In Merry's ear, she whispered, "I've missed you."

CHAPTER 24

◆——◆——◆

Otter

When the *Tempest* arrived at the dock, Otter had one of her fathers at her side, while the other steered the ship and her mother—the dragon—patrolled far, far from her natural territory.

What Otter didn't expect to see was the queen herself, there on the dock, waiting. She appeared to be alone and hidden in plain sight, but Otter recognized her when Queen Evangeline briefly pushed her hood back.

Otter quickly pulled her cloak around her shoulders and joined London and her fathers to go greet the queen.

"Captain Maul, I received your message," the queen said as she held her thick hood around her face again. "I see that you are hale, and your ship is mostly intact. I will deal with these . . . *pirates*. This will not stand!"

Before the captain could speak, an enormous wave arose, as if the sea itself was cresting. The queen flinched and erected a ward that shielded her—as well as Otter, London, Tanner, and Captain Maul—from harm.

They watched as the wave shaped itself into a pathway, a bridge from sea to dock. And on that bridge stood a woman in a dress made of shimmering fabric. It was more vibrant than the dragon-shed hide that made the Ravens' armor and sparkled more than the light that danced upon the sea. Her hair matched Otter's many-hued tresses, and her skin seemed to flicker in flashes of red, gold, and indigo as if she were created from mother-of-pearl.

"Why, you're a . . ." The queen looked at Marian in awe.

A small puff of fire came from Marian's lips as she completed the queen's sentence: "Dragon."

At that, she stepped through the queen's ward.

Queen Evangeline extended a hand. "I am honored . . ."

"Marian," the captain filled in. "This is Marian, mother to Tanner's and my little Ottilie. We met up with her after an accident at sea, but before the pirates."

Her dad sounded suspiciously emotional, and Otter glanced at him.

"Pirates in my waters!" The queen shook her head.

Marian looked at the queen as if to say, *Whose waters?* No one but Otter seemed to notice, though, and she shared a look with her human-shaped dragon mother.

Otter had to remind herself that this was real. She was standing next to her mother, and she had so many questions for her—especially now that Otter herself had switched into and out of dragon shape.

Marian reached out and squeezed Otter's hand. "We will have time."

Otter felt steadier than she ever had, even with dragon-hide cloaks. Maybe it was not the shed skin but the touch of another dragon's hand that she'd needed to feel steady on land.

"We shall deal with the pirates," Marian said. "And perhaps you can tell me what your plan is to address the hatchling problem."

"Hatchlings?" Queen Evangeline asked.

Just then, from the *Tempest's* deck, they could hear the Lost Ones arguing about keeping their spears "just in case."

Marian nodded to the children. "Hatchlings."

"Come on, then." Otter beckoned to them. "Join us! Leave your spears on the ship, where they will be safe."

Hearing that, the Lost Ones let their spears clatter to the ground, and they charged toward land. It wasn't Marian they clustered around, though. They were Otter's *friends* now. Maybe because she'd fished them out of the sea—and maybe because she was a kid, too.

In the cacophony of ten kids talking at once, Otter felt a little like when the kelpies got chatty—except this felt like a good kind of noise.

Her fathers were explaining, "The children stopped the pirates so the *Tempest* could sail to safety."

"Ottilie and our son, London"—the captain nodded at London—"led the charge on the pirates."

One of the Lost Ones said, "The pirates were hopping mad!"

"The frogs were a'hopping, too!" Berty chimed in with a demonstration of hopping.

Soon all the kids were hopping around, making a game of mimicking the pirates and frogs.

The queen stared at them. Her small gasp turned into a smothered chuckle when one of the Lost Ones yelled, in a rather poor imitation of the pirates, "Well, you've burned my bum, you *frog*."

Marian watched them fondly.

"Frogs, though?" the queen mused.

"Frogs," Otter confirmed before motioning her friends to her side.

"The children are why I am in this world," Marian told the queen, sounding as regal as she did when she was a massive, towering dragon-shaped being. "I have protected many of your hatchlings, but *all* hatchlings must have safety."

The queen nodded. "I agree, Lady Marian. My advisors are meeting with some of the children of Glass City right now to formulate plans."

"Good. Then I shan't have to eat you," Marian said, leaving the queen momentarily speechless.

"One *must* take care of hatchlings," Marian repeated. "Teach them. Feed them. Guard them. *Love* them. Ask your gargoyles. They know. Ask Ebba. They know, too."

At that, the Glass Queen smiled. "Yes, we are lucky to have the gargoyles—and even Ebba. There are many who care."

The queen looked at Otter and London. "Why, just today I met some young people you might like to meet. Why don't you all come to the palace?"

Otter looped an arm through her brother's, and with their friends and family, they set off onto land. She'd never felt so steady on dry land, and the thought that she could now explore the city was intriguing.

She was, after all, an adventurer whether she was in human shape or scaled.

And following Marian and Evangeline through the city *was* an adventure. No one but those nearest them realized that they were in the presence of dragons and queens—and children who would change the world.

Humans could be such odd creatures, Otter thought, not seeing what was right before them. But they were wonderful.

And the creatures in all worlds were dazzling. In the sea were dragons; in the Netherwhere were gargoyles and Ebba, and maybe even some dragonets she'd like to know better. Maybe she'd even chat with kelpies now that she wasn't so angry that *they* got to be in the water all the time.

Otter smiled. So many creatures to get to know, so many places she was lucky to belong. She was still a person meant for the sea—be it on a ship or in the waters!—but now she could *also* venture onto land.

She squeezed her brother's arm. Let the new adventures begin!

EPILOGUE

◆———◆———◆

Each time the door to the Netherwhere opened, the group of children tumbled in. They'd become a family of sorts, the young Nightshade, the thieves, and the princess. But here, they were neither dragon nor human, neither alchemist nor ward worker, neither royal nor thief, they were simply *hatchlings.*

They carried none of the responsibilities of their world with them. They simply frolicked as hatchlings were meant to do. The Netherwhere was their playground, and Marian took joy in seeing it—though not as much as *they* clearly did with their laughter and yelling.

"It's good," Ebba said from somewhere behind her. "I like that they still come even though they are safe over *there* now."

"It is," she agreed.

The importance of protecting hatchlings was the one thing Ebba and Marian agreed upon.

Ebba flopped onto the beach at her side. Their snake head shouted silly suggestions at the hatchlings. Their goat head giggled. But their lion head looked at Marian, who was in human shape just then.

"They're happy," Ebba's lion head said.

"All hatchlings ought to be." Marian looked at the children, currently playing some sort of slug-riding jousting game.

Gargoyles watched from trees, and the occasional faery flitted by. Laughter drew the Netherwhere beings to the edge of the sea.

No matter what shape they were, the truth of the matter was that there was one very good reason why children were welcome in the Netherwhere and *most* adults were not. The Netherwhere was the land of a chimera, of gargoyles, of faeries, and of dragons.

It was a place for beings who were special and capable of amazing things.

It was a place for magic.

And *every* child—every hatchling—is full of magic.

ACKNOWLEDGMENTS

Once upon a time, a younger version of me lived at the edge of a forest and dreamed of a life at sea. Uncle Charlie—who remains one of the most influential people in my life years after his passing—would stack my arms with Victorian novels and say, "Books are adventures for when you cannot travel." As if that wasn't gift enough, he would continue, "So tell me what would happen if . . ."

Years later, as a young mother, "what would happen if" was a game I played with my then-young son.

The adventure that I created in this book can be traced back to both Uncle Charlie and my eldest son, Dylan. You are the two men who inspired me to write this one.

I write because *story* was a part of my life as a child and as a mother. I write because there were books I wanted to read that weren't on the shelves. And my family said, *tell me*.

Telling isn't as easy if no one can hear you. For that, deep gratitude goes to my editor, Nancy. Without you, this book would still be on my old laptop, incomplete, and lost to wherever old laptop files go to die. Working with you has been life-altering.

And as awesome as Nancy is, *you* are also essential in making so many details work, Sara LaFleur. Thank you for the many things you do.

Vivienne To, when I look at this cover, I swear I can hear the sea and feel the breeze. Sometimes I look at my middle grade books and just sigh. They're *stunning* thanks to you.

To Merrilee, my agent of *fourteen years* now. Thank you for having my back when I need to face pirates or whatever else this job puts in my path.

And most of all, to my family. You never hesitate when I say, "I need water. River. Lake. Ocean." From sea excursions to kayaks, you are the best crew I could dream to find. My claws and fangs are *always* yours.